I0535933

OTHER TITLES BY STACEY JOY NETZEL

MUST LOVE DIAMONDS

Must Love Frosting

Love Loyal and True

Love You, Baby

To Love and Protect

Don't Dare a Diamond

ITALY INTRIGUE SERIES

*Kidnapped**

Betrayed

Conned

*2012 Write Touch Readers' Award Winner as *Lost in Italy*

COLORADO TRUST SERIES

Evidence of Trust

Trust by Design

Trust in the Lawe

Shattered Trust

Dare to Trust

Vow of Trust

Illusion of Trust

WELCOME TO REDEMPTION SERIES

A Fair to Remember, Book 2

Grounds For Change, Book 4

The Heart of the Matter, Book 6

Hold On To Me, Book 8

Say You'll Marry Me, Book 10

(books 1,3,5,7,9 written by Donna Marie Rogers)

ROMANCING WISCONSIN SERIES

Mistletoe Mischief

Mistletoe Magic

Mistletoe Match-up

**Mistletoe Rules* – short bonus story

Autumn Wish

Autumn Bliss

Autumn Kiss

**Autumn Glimmer* – short bonus story

Spring Fling

Spring Serendipity

Spring Dreams

**Spring Spark* – short bonus story

Summer Scandal

Summer Bride

"Do you remember my niece from Texas?"

Reyes's smile faltered. *Raine Diamond.* A woman impossible to forget—even though he'd tried over the past ten months.

"I remember her," he confirmed cautiously.

"She took a bad spill recently and has been having some issues with her horse ever since," Mark said. "My brother asked if you'd be willing to work with them."

His pulse skipped, and he had to fight to keep his expression neutral. They'd gotten along about as well as oil and water. "I work with horses, not people."

"They're a package deal."

"Then I'm not your guy."

The senator shrugged. "My niece is used to getting her way, and it's not working with her current trainer. They're running out of time to qualify for the Olympic team and Matt's desperate."

Her dad was desperate? Not her? Great. And if he didn't produce results, what then?

Didn't matter. He didn't do package deals, and he wasn't going to Texas. "I'm sorry, but you know I can't leave right now with Dad gone."

"That's why she's coming here."

Well, shit. "When?"

The senator checked his watch before digging into his pocket to pull out a set of keys and a slip of paper. "She'll be here by six."

PRAISE FOR STACEY JOY NETZEL'S OTHER WORK

"A funny, sexy, hot romance that you won't want to put down." ~ Cerbes, for **MUST LOVE FROSTING**

"I truly adored reading it! It's a feel-good, sexy & moving romance." ~ Doni, for **LOVE LOYAL AND TRUE**

"I figured if anyone could write a story like this and win me over, it would be this author. And believe me, Stacey did not disappoint. I highly recommend [**LOVE YOU, BABY**] as well as the rest of the Must Love Diamonds series." ~ Elizabeth, Amazon Reviewer

"Fantastic! Shelby and Dev's story is loaded with drama, humor, sizzle, action and suspense." ~ Deb D, Amazon reviewer for **TO LOVE AND PROTECT**

"The **Romancing Wisconsin Series** is fantastic...the characters are amazing and the plots make you want to keep reading straight through." ~ Debbie, Amazon reviewer

Summer Secrets

Summer Wager – short-ish bonus story

STAND ALONE ROMANCE TITLES

More Than a Kiss, contemporary romance

Chasin' Mason, contemporary western romance

Ditched Again, high school reunion novella

Dragonfly Dreams, Christmas novella

Nina, Beach Brides sweet contemporary novella

PARANORMAL ROMANCE TITLES

If Tombstones Could Talk, paranormal novella

Beneath Still Waters (Part One), paranormal novella

Rising Above (Still Waters Part Two), paranormal novella

FREE READ

Holding Out For a Hero

PUZZLE BOOK

Passion & Puzzles

a Word Search and Crossword Puzzle Book of Stacey Joy
Netzel Romance books

Don't Dare a diamond

BOOK 5

MUST LOVE DIAMONDS

BY
STACEY JOY NETZEL

Don't Dare a Diamond

Must Love Diamonds Series, book 5

Copyright © 2020, Stacey Joy Netzel

Editor: Stacy D. Holmes

Cover Art: Cover Couture

ebook ISBN: 9781939143815

Print ISBN: 9781939143822

Nikki -

You know how they say you can pick your friends but not your family? Well, if we weren't family, I'd still pick you.

I am so thankful to have you (and the rest of your family) in my life.

Love you always!

July
Lakewood, CO

Raine Diamond wasn't used to being ignored. She may be twenty-five, but she was still the baby of her family, *and* the only girl out of five kids. She'd graduated valedictorian of her high school class, and summa cum laude from the University of Texas.

She was a world-class show jumper, having already won a gold medal in the Youth Olympic Games at eighteen, with aspirations of making the U.S. Olympic team in the near future. Possibly even next year. Her grandfather was a real estate mogul, her parents ran a multi-billion dollar investment firm, and one uncle was a senator, the other head of a jewelry empire.

She was a *Diamond*.

And what was he? A stable boy.

Well…man. A stable *man* who made her pulse race like never before—and that scared the crap out of her.

She fidgeted with the seam on the back pocket of her jeans as she stood in her uncle's kitchen with her cousin, Shelby, her brother, Axel, and Reyes Torrez.

She didn't usually act like an entitled little rich bitch, but for some reason, Reyes triggered the need to prove she was worth looking at. By him. But while her heart went completely haywire at the sight of his thick-lashed green eyes and sun-kissed, caramel-colored hair, he gave her a cool, heat-inducing once-over, met her gaze long enough for her to offer a nervous smile, and then dismissed her without a second glance.

As he easily joked and laughed with her cousin and brother, she battled a foreign insecurity that left her confused and annoyed. Then he left without so much as a, *"Nice to meet you."*

Who was *he* to act as if she didn't even exist?

If he'd been into Shelby, she'd have understood. Heck, even if he had a girlfriend, he could've simply been pleasantly polite. That's what people did when they met someone new—or were reintroduced after nearly ten years. But the way he'd openly ignored her had been an outright snub. The more she thought about it, the more offended she became.

She stewed all through brunch, only briefly distracted when her cousin Merit dropped a bombshell on the whole family that he and his girlfriend, Mae, were having a baby. Apparently, the girlfriend part had been news, too?

Uncle Mark didn't take it well, and after a dramatic argument, Merit stormed out, Mae followed, then Aunt Janine. After the meal came to an awkward end, her brothers and cousins and their significant others cleared the table and did dishes before settling back around the patio. While they discussed the drama and caught up, she couldn't stop glaring across the lawn toward the stables.

After a few minutes, she got up and wandered inside the house. They were staying one more night, so she'd have plenty of time for visiting, but right now she was restless. Bored with the conversation around the table—and irritated by repeated flashes of Reyes' rude slight.

If only she hadn't sent Diamond Fire home to Texas with their trainer. After they'd won their event yesterday, he'd more than earned a few days rest at home, but now she couldn't go down to the stables with the excuse of checking on her champion baby.

Seeing her mom and Aunt Janine coming down the stairs, Raine seized on a different idea. "Aunt Jan, would it be possible for me to borrow one of your horses for an hour or so?" She rarely went a day without riding, but she couldn't remember the last time she'd been on the back of a horse just for fun.

"Of course." Her aunt gave her a distracted smile,

clearly still focused on the earlier brunch drama. "Just ask Estefan or Reyes who could use some exercise."

Her pulse skipped at the mention of the second name. "Thank you."

She hurried upstairs to change and tucked her black V-neck T-shirt into tan breeches before pulling on black, knee-high, leather riding boots. She felt a little bad not asking Shelby to go with her, but her cousin knew her too well and would see right through this move.

When she reached the stables a few minutes later, she had a hard time catching her breath, and it had nothing to do with her speed walk down the curvy driveway. As she approached the open doors, her heart lodged in her throat, and a mass of anxiety writhed in her stomach. She desperately wanted to see him, yet also hoped he was nowhere around, because really, what was she going to say?

Notice me.

Yeah, that wouldn't sound pathetic and self-centered at all.

She stepped inside the barn and scanned for Reyes, only to find the place deserted. Initial relief was quickly replaced by disappointment, until she realized just because she didn't see him didn't mean he wasn't around. Shelby had said he lived in an apartment above the barn.

Squaring her shoulders, she held her chin high as she ventured farther inside. Like at home, the aisles were immaculate, and a deep inhale filled her lungs with

4

the beloved scents of horse, hay, and leather. Heads turned her way, delicate ears swiveling and perking up as pairs of curious brown eyes watched her approach.

She stopped in front of a stall halfway down the aisle and studied the bay thoroughbred inside. The gelding's shiny coat was a rich red, complimented by a silky, jet-black forelock, mane, and tail. He was a big boy like Fire, his withers the same height as her five feet, two inches, putting him at almost sixteen hands tall.

He turned his head with a soft whicker, and she stepped back when he moved forward to extend his head over the stall door. She let him sniff her hand, then stroked his neck as he lipped at her palm.

"Hello, gorgeous." While rubbing his forehead and laying her cheek against his velvety soft black muzzle, she glanced at the engraved name plate on his stall door.

RazMaTaz.

"Tell me big guy, do they call you Raz, or Taz?" she mused out loud.

"That's Taz."

Her breath caught as she whirled around to see an older gentleman step through a door off to her right. He carried an English saddle over one arm, and a bridle in the other hand.

"Raine?"

"That's me," she confirmed with a smile.

"Hi. I'm Estefan. Janine called and said you were looking for a mount."

Earlier, she'd heard Shelby tell Merit's girlfriend

5

Estefan was Reyes' father. She could also see the resemblance to his son in his olive-toned features and brown eyes from their Spanish heritage. The elder Torrez had a mustache peppered with gray in comparison to his son's neatly trimmed goatee.

"Can I ride him?" she asked hopefully as she stroked the bay's nose. Forget going for a trail ride, she'd love to see what the horse could do on a course.

"Taz is my son's horse," he advised with a hint of apology in his tone. "No one rides him but Reyes."

She blinked in surprise to learn he had his own horse here. None of their employees kept their horses at the Diamond stables in Texas. Not to mention, the gelding looked to be easily worth twenty grand. Maybe more.

"I'll be saddling Stimpy for you. He could use some exercise."

Stimpy?

Did he not know what she did for a living? She smoothed out her wrinkled nose as she turned, anticipating an old, gentle gelding for beginners.

Estefan slid the stall door open, giving Raine a good look at a regal chestnut with a mass of wavy, reddish-brown mane. Smaller than Taz, the more delicate build and refined features pointed toward Arabian, and she grinned with anticipation. Okay, she could definitely live with Stimpy—which upon a closer look at his nameplate, looked to be short for Rumplestiltskin.

"Your aunt assures me you can handle some fire?"

"Of course." She gave Taz a final, longing stroke

6

along his muzzle before crossing the aisle. "I've been riding my Trakhener, Diamond Fire, since I was seventeen, and I can assure you, he lives up to his name."

He nodded, clearly well-versed with the athletic attributes of her jumper's breed.

"Is it okay for me to take Stimpy out on the trails? Just for an hour or so."

"You remember them?" he asked with an arch of his brows.

"I do. I know it's been a while," she said with a shrug, "but as long as they haven't changed…"

"No, no changes," he assured her. "Warm him up in the arena, get a feel for how he handles, and you should be good."

He wasn't telling her anything she didn't know, but she nodded anyway. "Thanks."

Used to taking care of her own mounts, she stepped forward to saddle the gelding, but Estefan would hear nothing of it. Minutes later, he gave her a leg up and a few tips on the Arabian's personality, then left them with, "Enjoy your ride."

She didn't remember him.

Reyes knew the moment Raine Diamond gave him that warm, interested smile up at the main house, she didn't remember treating him like a smear of manure on the heels of her polished English riding boots during a summer visit ten years ago. His sixteen year old ego had taken a hit, but the memory of two fifteen year old girls drooling over his older brother wasn't what rekindled his resentment after all this time.

It was the fact she hadn't even seen him back then. Dev had been twenty at the time, home on military leave, enjoying his R&R at the pool while hanging out with Loyal and Asher. Reyes had been invisible down in the stables, mucking stalls, sweeping aisles, stacking hay. Fine, he had a job to do. But when he'd finished his shift and joined the rest of 'em, the pretty, brunette Diamond cousin hadn't given him the time of day as she pranced around in her little red bikini.

To her, he'd just been a stable boy. The hired help who'd been shoveling manure while she and Bells went for a joy ride earlier that morning. Of all the years he'd grown up hanging with the Diamond kids, even knowing the gulf of privilege that separated their families, he'd never once felt less than any one of them— until that day.

That feeling came roaring back again today. Didn't matter that he'd caught a flare of interest in the now twenty-five year old's hazel eyes, it was the knowing she didn't recall snubbing him that hit the hardest. To her, he hadn't even been worth remembering.

The irony of that pissing him off was a real kick in the ass. These days, he *wanted* to fade into the background. Since getting out of the Army almost a year ago and coming home, he made sure his usual happy-go-lucky smile and carefree attitude kept everyone from seeing all the shit he kept bottled up inside.

The only one who suspected how deep it went was Dev, but ninety-nine percent of the time he was training or on a mission, so other than the occasional email or text, he left him alone. The horses were his mental therapy, and with the stables relatively quiet now that the senator and Janine spent a lot of time in Washington, he'd been virtually invisible and glad for it.

One look at Raine up at the main house had set his nerve endings buzzing with energy. His grip tightened on the windowsill of his above-the-stables apartment window as he watched her out in the arena astride Stimpy. Her slim form moved as one with the horse, her long hair streaming out behind her as she cantered him in figure eights with a firm hold on the reins.

The chestnut Arabian could be a headstrong sonofabitch, but right now, he moved willingly under her guidance, his lead switches smooth as butter. Reyes couldn't help but be impressed by her skill and grace in the saddle, though it wasn't surprising given he'd heard Shelby bragging she was in the running for a spot on the US Equestrian Team.

When she exited the arena for the riding trails surrounding the estate, he headed down to the stables. His gut clenched as his mind screamed to turn around and go back. It reminded him of being on patrol. Trouble was brewing, and he was heading right for it. But he could no more have kept himself from descending the stairs than he could've disobeyed an order from his commanding officer.

The certainty of that left him itchy and restless, and he needed to do something with his hands. In Afghanistan, he used to clean his rifle, and then clean it again. Now, he'd have to make do with saddles. It was almost as good.

In the tack room, he grabbed a cloth and some leather cleaner.

His dad walked by, then back-tracked. Reyes looked up when he stopped in the doorway. "You headed out?"

"Not quite. I'm waiting for Janine's niece to get back from her ride."

"Is Mom done with everything up at the house?" They always rode together when his mom worked on Sundays.

His dad shrugged. "She'll keep herself busy until I can leave."

"You can go if you want. I'll take care of things here."

"Got nothing better to do on your day off?"

Reyes lifted a shoulder as he avoided making eye contact. "I'm heading out later, so just killing some time for now."

"Hmm." His dad watched him quietly for a moment.

His pulse thudded hard as he waited to be called out on the lie.

Instead, his dad gave a shrug. "All right then, suit yourself. Thanks."

It didn't suit him one damn bit, yet there he sat, scrubbing the already shining leather until the light sound of boot heels beat out a rapid rhythm on the cement twenty minutes later. He went on full alert as the steps came to an abrupt halt outside the tack room door.

"Oh. Um…is Estefan here?"

Reyes took his time looking up, partly to make her wait, partly to get his pulse to settle down. But one look at Raine's windblown hair and those bright hazel eyes, and there was no reprieve in sight. "He went home. Why?"

"I was hoping to get some jumps set up."

"Sure." He gestured to the left with the oil cloth in his hand. "Out the main doors, you'll find a large storage room on the left. Jumps are in there. Help yourself."

She blinked at him, her expression astonished. "Help myself?"

"Yep. Just make sure you keep them under half a meter. Stimpy doesn't have nearly the same level of training as your jumpers."

One hand propped on her hip, and her brow arched imperiously as her cheeks flushed with color. "You do work here, don't you?"

"I do."

Her gaze narrowed, and he deliberately returned to polishing.

"And you aren't going to at least come help me?"

"I'm busy."

After a long moment, she pivoted on her heel and disappeared toward the storage room. Reyes rested his fist on the saddle with a heavy sigh, waiting for the sound of the wooden rails as she dragged them out to the arena. When all he heard was silence, he conceded maybe he didn't have to be such an asshole because his pansy-ass ego was still bruised from ten years ago. Maybe he should go help—

The clip-clop of horseshoes rang out on the cement.

His brow dipped as he rose and walked to the doorway in time to see Raine leading Stimpy to the cross ties by his assigned stall. She didn't deign to look in his direction as they passed the tack room.

Leaning a shoulder against the doorjamb, he asked, "Change your mind about the jumping?"

"Shelby texted me to meet her at the pool."

Her snooty tone grated across his nerves while his fingers clenched the cloth in his hand at the memory of that little red bikini all those years ago. A mental head-shake banished the image as she secured the gelding in the cross ties. Then she gave him a rub on the nose and flipped her hair over her shoulder while turning to walk toward the main house.

Reyes couldn't help but drop his gaze down to the sway of her ass in those tan, skin-tight pants. He swallowed hard against a rising tide of awareness.

"Tell your dad thank you for the ride," she tossed over her shoulder while bending to fish her phone from the front thigh pocket of her breeches.

Reyes tilted his head slightly to watch the stretch of material—until he suddenly straightened from the wall with a jerk of indignation. "Whoa—hold on. Where the hell do you think you're going?"

"To the pool, of course."

"Not before you take care of Stimpy."

"I do believe that's what *you're* paid to do. I'm going to go have a swim."

It was, and it wasn't, but he wasn't about to get into semantics with an uppity little princess like her. "*You're* going to get your ass back here and take care of this horse. Now."

That halted her steps and brought her back around. She lifted her chin, somehow looking down her nose at him from twenty feet away. "You can't talk to me like that. I'll have you fired."

He snorted. "Good luck with that. In the meantime, the rule is, you ride in this stable, you take care of your horse. You may not remember everything about this place, but I know damn well you remember that."

"What does that mean?"

Annoyed with himself for revealing his resentment, he abruptly turned and went back into the tack room.

"I'll have you fired."

The echo of her threat had him clenching his jaw, but he forced himself to take a seat behind the saddle he'd been cleaning and focus on the rhythmic motions of his hand to soothe his pissed-off energy.

While his anger eased, a strange crackle and buzz

13

woke up every cell of his body. The level shot up a notch when, five minutes later, she stomped into the room to deposit Stimpy's saddle and bridle on an empty rack and hook without so much as a glance in his direction. Then she went straight to the bins on the other side of the room, selected the brushes she needed to rub the horse down, and stomped back out again.

See? He shot a narrow-eyed look at the empty doorway. She hadn't forgotten where the brushes were located, and after today, he'd bet a hundred bucks she'd remember him the next time they met.

It could be a year, or another ten, but she'd definitely remember him.

2

*ay - 10 months later
Dallas, TX*

Raine leaned forward slightly in the saddle, heels down as she counted Diamond Fire's strides on their approach to the next jump, a vertical with two rails, one-point-two-five meters high. They could do this jump in their sleep—except her shoulders tensed and body stiffened as the nightmare of their fall during the final event of last season flashed in her mind with sickening clarity.

Fire tossed his head and stumbled a step. When he regained his footing, she wheeled him to the left, and they galloped past the jump with her heart lodged in her throat.

"It's okay," her trainer called from the center of the

15

arena. "Take him around and try it again. You'll get it on this round."

Charlie's encouraging claps echoed up into the steel rafters, but she could hear the tight edge of dissatisfaction eating into his patience. He wanted results. Because her dad paid him an obscene amount of money for those results, and the pressure was on for all of them.

She didn't need to glance toward the tall, blond trainer in the arena to know his sharp blue gaze was analyzing her every move. Anxiety spiked her pulse, and she cantered Fire past the next jump, too.

"Stop pushing so hard," she snapped. "I told you he's not ready yet."

"It's been four and a half months, Raine."

"Four and a half months and he's still stumbling on an easy jump."

He propped one hand on his hip as he gestured toward the course with his other. "He did okay when Jess rode him while your shoulder healed."

"So it's all my fault?" She pointed her baby toward a pathetically low, single vertical. On Fire's way over, one nick of his back hoof bounced the rail from the cups. "How about that? Was that my fault, too?"

"He can sense your anxiety. He—"

"*I'm* fine," she hollered from the far end of the arena.

"—knows you don't trust him."

"He doesn't trust *me*," she shot back, nausea threatening to send up her breakfast from two hours ago.

Tears of frustration burned her eyes as she reined Fire to a stop in front of their trainer. Ever since the accident, nothing had been the same between her and her horse. Their perfect partnership had crashed into the dirt right alongside them that day at the end of December. Eight years down the drain. And now Charlie kept throwing it in her face—just like her dad.

"You gotta get this jump back if you're going to compete at your previous level," Charlie said, his tone firm, yet sympathetic. "You were almost disqualified last week."

Her stomach roiled as she recalled how bad their ride had gone at the event. They hadn't racked up that many faults in years. "You're not telling me anything I don't already know. And I certainly don't need to hear it every damn day."

A tiny voice whispered she wasn't so sure she wanted to keep competing, but she didn't dare listen. She hated the sliver of doubt that kept surfacing at the worst times. Jumping was her life. It had been since her first show when she was nine. If she wasn't riding, she didn't know who she was, or what the hell else she'd do.

She gripped the reins tighter to keep her hands from shaking. Fire danced backward until she relaxed her hold.

Charlie heaved a resigned sigh and gave a slight shake of his head. "Cool him down and then do your workout. We'll give it another go tomorrow."

Raine swung Fire around and posted as he trotted

one circuit of the ring, then slowed him to a walk for a couple more rounds. Finally, she dismounted and led him from the arena into the attached stable while unstrapping her helmet. After removing his saddle and bridle, she gave him a thorough rub down before gathering the tack to put away.

"You're not pushing her hard enough."

The sound of her father's angry voice pulled her up short two steps from the tack room door.

"*She* complains I'm pushing her too hard," Charlie argued.

"She walks all over you, and we both know it. If she doesn't get back to competition level, she won't have time to qualify."

Raine grit her teeth, so sick of the two of them getting on her case about the Olympics. What did they want her to do, force Fire over the jumps? He'd really hate her then.

"I keep telling her that," her trainer told her dad.

"And then you let her off the hook and cut practice short."

"I'm doing my best."

"Then your best isn't good enough. She needs better. Different."

Impatience dripped from her dad's voice. She could picture the two of them facing off, her dad's dark, brooding expression challenging the younger man's.

"I'm sending her and Diamond Fire up to my brother's in Denver for the next month."

What?

Raine stiffened at her dad's words. That was news to her.

"Am I being fired?" Charlie asked.

"Of course not. You'll stay here to work with the alternates while they head up north. A change of scenery will do them both some good, and my brother has a trainer who works wonders with their rescue horses."

Indignation spurred her around the corner to confront her dad. "Fire isn't some broken down rescue horse."

He didn't seem the least bit concerned she'd been eavesdropping. "No, but he does need some work. You both do."

"Which we can do here." She hugged the saddle tighter against her churning stomach. "I'm not going to Uncle Mark's."

He crossed his arms over his chest, dark eyebrows rising toward dark hair just beginning to gray at the temples. "Yes, you are."

"I'll miss two events."

"After where you finished last week, that's the least of our worries."

"Dad."

"Raine, it's not up for discussion."

It took everything she had to not stamp her foot like when she was five and didn't get her way. "Fire and I will be fine. We *are* making progress. We just need more time."

He shook his head. "You don't have time. If you have any hope of making the Olympic team, you have to get back to where you were."

Those damn tears threatened again as she choked out, "We will."

Her dad put his hands on her shoulders, the weight of them as heavy as his voice. "Honey, you've talked about going for gold since you were ten. I told you I'd help you get there, and that's exactly what I'm doing." He pulled her in for a quick hug. With her tucked in under his chin, he dropped a kiss on the top of her head before setting her back with a firm grip. "You leave first thing in the morning. Pack for a month."

She sputtered furiously as he strode away, even though she knew from that tone, nothing she said would change his mind. She should've known he wouldn't let her stonewall Charlie forever.

The trainer gave her a helpless shrug before following her father. She growled under her breath as they both disappeared.

Alone in the tack room, Raine sank down onto a bench seat near the wall, saddle hugged tight to her stomach.

Shit. She was going back to Denver.

It wasn't just that she'd have to work with a new trainer she didn't know, but she'd have to face that arrogant jerk at Uncle Mark's stable again. She wished she didn't remember his name. Or the color of his eyes, the way his shirt had molded his broad shoulders, or how her pulse had tripped each time they came face to face.

But she did remember Reyes Torrez. All too well.

He'd featured in numerous girlish fantasies since she was fifteen, and a few more since she'd seen him again last summer. She could hope he'd been fired for some other jackass thing he'd done since then, but given the history between his family and Uncle Mark's, that was nothing more than a pipe dream.

3

Reyes was bent over checking Morning Glory's horseshoes when the sound of approaching footsteps had him glancing under his arm. He released the mare's foot and straightened to face the senator—also his boss. "Afternoon, Mark. I thought you and Janine were heading back to Washington today."

"We're on our way out, but I needed to come ask a personal favor before I left."

"Sure. Name it." He glanced past his shoulder to see their town car waiting beyond the open doors, their driver and bodyguard leaning against the front passenger door.

"First of all, I'm going to hold you to that," the senator said with a grin as he stroked his palm along the thoroughbred's neck. "Second, in the future, you might want to hear the favor before you agree to it."

Reyes returned his smile. "That's an ominous warning coming from a politician."

Mark chuckled. "So true. Anyway, do you remember my niece from Texas who visited last year? She came down to the barn for a ride?"

Now his smile faltered. *Raine Diamond.* A woman impossible to forget—even though he'd tried over the past ten months.

Following her progress on the jumping circuit is not *trying.*

Whatever.

"I remember her," he confirmed cautiously.

"She took a bad spill at the end of last season and got banged up pretty bad."

Yeah, he'd read about her fall and resulting shoulder surgery. And while she should've had plenty of time to heal, she and her champion Trakehner had faulted to the bottom of the board at the first two competitions of the season.

Despite their adversarial encounter last summer, he had sympathy for her—in a general sense, nothing more.

"Sorry to hear that," he murmured.

Mark gave a solemn nod. "She's recovered physically, but she's been having some issues with her horse ever since. My brother called yesterday and asked if you'd be willing to work with them."

His pulse skipped at the request, and he had to fight

to keep his expression neutral. "I work with horses, not people."

"They're a package deal."

"Then I'm not your guy."

"I told Matt what you've done with Janine's rescue horses, and he seems to think you'd be perfect."

Reyes frowned in confusion. "Based solely on your word?"

"Well, he is my brother." A small smile curved his boss' lips. "And he also overheard you stand up to Raine last summer."

Oh, shit, seriously? Heat flashed through him at the thought of her father overhearing that exchange. He'd been blunt and rude to knock her down off her high horse, but he'd have kept his mouth shut if he'd known anyone else was around. Maybe.

Knowing Mark knew about their encounter heaped on yet another level of discomfort—although, if it had been a problem, he wouldn't still have a job. "After that, I'd think I'm the last person he'd want working with his daughter."

The senator shrugged. "My niece is used to getting her way, and it's not working with her current trainer."

"Shocker," he muttered before he could help himself.

"Considering she was nearly disqualified last week, and they're running out of time to make sure she can qualify for the Olympic team, Matt's desperate."

Her dad was desperate? Not her? Great. And if he didn't produce results, what then?

Didn't matter. He didn't do package deals, and he wasn't going to Texas.

His parents had left for a month-long European tour and cruise five days ago. Which moved him up from assistant stable manager, to manager—because he was currently the *only* stable employee on the payroll. "Mark, I'm sorry, but you know I can't leave right now with Dad and Mom gone."

"That's why she's coming here."

Well, shit. "When?"

The senator glanced at his watch before digging into his pocket to pull out a set of keys and a slip of paper. "She'll be here about six."

"*Tonight?*"

"Like I said, they're running out of time." He held out the items in his hand, his smile somewhat apologetic. "Call Matt for the details, and give these keys to Raine, please. Janine made up the guest house, stocked the fridge, and left her Benz in the garage down there for her to use."

Reyes hesitated before releasing a sigh of resignation. "I don't even have the option to say no, do I?"

"I did tell you I was going to hold you to your initial acceptance."

He gave a grim smile and took the paper and keys from the older man's hand. "Lesson learned."

Mark clapped him on the back before heading out.

25

"Thanks, Rey. You got one month to fix what you can. Don't let me down."

Just a personal favor, hey? No pressure.

Sonofabitch.

As the senator slipped into the back seat of his car by his wife and their driver/bodyguard shut the door, Reyes fisted the keys in his hand. So much for the trail ride he'd planned on Taz. Now he had three hours to prepare for Her Royal Highness.

Scowling down at the slip of paper crumpled around the keys, he reached for his phone.

Reyes' pulse sped up when the luxury transport trailer pulled in two hours and forty-seven minutes later. *Nothing but the best for a Diamond.* With one shoulder braced against one of the massive vertical support beams that bracketed the barn doorway, he shoved his hands in his front pockets.

He didn't miss the glance Raine shot in his direction as she climbed down from the front passenger seat, but she went straight to the back, followed by a guy he assumed was a groom. He was kind of surprised to even see her in the truck when she could've taken a two-hour non-stop flight from Dallas and caught a cab to the estate—or called one of her cousins.

The driver got out and busied himself unloading five

large suitcases from the cargo compartment. When he dragged out a couple of tack trunks, a dozen bales of hay and three sacks of grain, Reyes stepped forward. He wasn't about to play bellhop for Princess Raine, but helping with the horse's necessities fit his job description.

He transferred the trunks to the empty stall next to the one he'd prepared for her gelding, then made his way around to the back of the trailer when there was still no sign of her or the horse. The doors were open, ramp down, but Raine and her horse were still inside.

While she murmured in a low voice and tugged on the gelding's lead rope, he took a moment to appreciate the view. After skimming his gaze over her slim figure in a white T-shirt, skinny jeans cuffed above the ankle, and white canvas tennis shoes, he forced his attention to her horse.

Diamond Fire. Though he'd seen the gelding in videos of her events online, the sleek, black-bay Trakehner was even more impressive in person. He knew the jumper sported three white socks under his leg wraps, and had a distinctive flame-shaped marking under his ebony forelock. Standing about sixteen hands high, the top of Raine's head barely reached his withers. A tall horse for a petite woman, yet in every video he'd watched, they made a perfect pair.

"You two coming out, or what?" Reyes asked.

Raine started at the sound of his voice, but didn't bother glancing his way. "When we're ready," she advised in a cool tone, her dark, wavy hair curtaining her face.

It didn't appear they were doing anything other than just standing there. He let another minute pass before giving voice to mounting impatience. "Maybe you don't have anything better to do, but I'm already two hours past quitting time."

"Then go," she snapped. "I didn't ask you to stay."

"No, but your uncle did. What's the hold up?"

She huffed out a sigh, shoulders drooping slightly. "He's being stubborn."

He frowned. "Is this normal for him?"

A shake of her head sent a ripple through her silky waves. "No. But then again, there's not much that's been normal lately."

The frustration in her voice sparked sympathy. He knew how it felt to miss normal, though his experience stemmed from an entirely different situation, and things had begun to improve this past year.

Marginally.

Setting that aside, he stepped up onto the ramp. "May I?"

Raine twisted around to glare at him, as if offended he dared to ask. Just as he was trying not to notice the pretty color of her hazel irises, she rolled her eyes and moved back while extending one hand with the lead rope in silent invitation. Clearly, she didn't expect him to succeed where she'd failed.

Or maybe, she *was* as desperate as her father.

Reyes entered the trailer, murmuring softly, keeping his gaze locked on Diamond Fire while taking the rope and easing closer to approach the horse from the side so he wouldn't startle him. Conscious of Raine watching with her arms crossed, he reached a hand to stroke the gelding's neck, then held his palm out for him to smell.

"Hey, boy, how's it going? I bet you're tired after the trip here, so how about we get you out of this box? The sun's still shining, and there's a nice, cool breeze outside."

He kept his voice low and smooth. The horse's ears flicked back and forth, then stayed forward as he arched his neck and turned to bump his forehead against Reyes' chest. When he leaned his weight into him, Reyes took a step back. The gelding turned to follow.

"There you go. Good boy." Forcing away a triumphant grin, he gave a gentle pull on the lead and led him toward the ramp. "Come on. We've got a clean stall all set for you, big guy."

Raine muttered, "Traitor," under her breath as they passed. At the bottom of the ramp, she stepped forward and took the lead rope from his hands. "I'm going to walk him around to stretch his legs."

He lifted his palms and stepped away—but not before he caught a whiff of something light and flowery. The enticing scent amped up his pulse all over again. "I'll meet you inside when you're ready."

As she led her horse away, the groom and driver were already closing up the trailer to leave. Reyes stood by the barn as they drove away, leaving Raine's pile of luggage and horse feed stacked by the front doors. Looked like he'd be playing bellhop after all. He gave a low growl, then set to work transferring the hay and grain into the same stall as her trunks.

Nearly fifteen minutes later, the clip-clop of hooves drew him out of the office next to the stable's tack room. He made his way down the aisle to show Raine the stall he'd prepared for Diamond Fire, and the one next to it where he'd stored all the tack and feed.

"How's he doing?"

"He's fine," she said shortly. "I don't know what got into him. He's never done that before."

Reyes didn't know what to say to make her feel better about the horse's refusal to obey. It wasn't like the two of them weren't used to travelling for events and being in new places on a regular basis, so he couldn't blame it on that. He also didn't quite know why he wanted to ease her distress, so he kept silent as she put the gelding in the stall and checked everything over.

When he noticed her intense scrutiny of every nook and cranny, a spark of defensive annoyance surged forward. "Everything up to your standards, your Highness?"

The sarcasm earned him a sideways glare. "It's fine," she said. "You can go now."

Oh, how badly he wanted to be an asshole after such a haughty dismissal. Instead, he gave her a smile that he hoped irked the shit out of her. "Come on now, I know you don't *really* want me to leave."

A flash of alarm lit her hazel eyes a second before she scoffed and arched her brows. "Wanna bet?"

"Wanna carry all that luggage to the guest house by yourself?"

Her gaze cut to the door where the transport driver had left her things in a jumbled pile. She clenched her jaw a second before her shoulders slumped. "No."

"I'll give you five minutes to finish up, and then I'll drive you over."

"I'm not quite ready to leave Fire yet. Just leave everything at the door, and I'll walk over when I'm finished."

He had to give her credit for that one—not for ordering him around like her own personal servant, but for taking care of her horse. She looked exhausted after the twelve-hour drive from Texas, and if he was honest, he'd totally expected her to bail on the animal.

"Suit yourself." He pulled out the keys the senator had given him. "These are for the house. Janine filled the fridge and left her car in the garage for you to use, so you should be all set."

"Thanks." Her tone was grudging as she accepted the keys. Then she looked around as if searching for someone. After a long moment, she asked, "Did my uncle say anything to your dad about what's going on? No one's bothered to inform me who I'm supposed to be working with, or when we're supposed to meet. I expected him—or her—to be here tonight."

Reyes blinked. She didn't know *he* was her new trainer for the next month?

No, of course not. After all, he was nothing more than a stable boy. It wouldn't even cross her mind that he might be more than just the guy who shoveled shit for the senator.

This was going to be interesting.

4

With her running shoes pounding the pavement, Raine made the final turn off the road, back into her aunt and uncle's long, paved driveway a little after seven a.m. the next morning. She didn't usually work out until after jump practice, but being cooped up in the transport truck yesterday left her restless and full of pent-up energy.

It was cooler up here in Colorado than Texas, and the Rocky Mountains made a beautiful backdrop in the bright sunlight. If only the gorgeous scenery made a difference. Usually, a run helped her relax and decompress, but this morning, thoughts of Reyes Torrez dominated every step of the way.

She shot a glance toward the barn. Last night, his vehicle had been parked outside the doors again when she left Fire, and when she glanced back, she'd noticed lights on in the apartment above the stables. With her

33

aunt and uncle back in Washington, she'd been mildly relieved she wasn't alone at the estate, yet also disturbed to realize the man taking up so much of her mind space lived so close by.

Yesterday, she'd hated admitting to him she didn't know what the hell was going on. She hated even more the smug little grin that had tugged at the corners of his mouth, as if knowing something she didn't was highly amusing to him. She hated most that when she'd fallen into bed, she'd dreamed about both smacking the smile off his face *and* kissing it off.

It made no sense that she was attracted to a man so wholly infuriating. She'd erroneously figured sleep would give her a reprieve from thinking about him.

"My dad's gone for the next three weeks," Reyes had informed her last night. *"Which means I'm in charge. Your trainer will be here at eight a.m. sharp. Don't be late."*

Even though she had plenty of time, she increased her stride past the stables and headed toward the guest house to take a shower and grab a quick breakfast.

"I'm in charge."

His firm tone when he said those words made her hate that fact as much as everything else. If his, *"Don't be late,"* were any indication, the jerk would probably be a major pain in her ass on purpose. He was already halfway there after getting Fire to follow him out of the trailer like he was the Pied Piper.

Reyes had stalked away last night before she could

ask any more questions. Like, *who exactly is this magical, secret trainer my dad thinks will fix everything?*

Why are you such a jerk?

Do you have a girlfriend?

Nope, skip that last one. She didn't need to know, because it didn't matter one bit. She was here for work, not to be distracted by the sexy stable guy. If only Dad had given her the details of this month-long exile instead of making himself scarce so she couldn't hound him about it and change his mind. And with Mom in Vancouver on a business trip, she'd been no help.

Raine hurried through her shower, ate a quick bowl of oatmeal and fresh fruit, and then braided her long, damp hair so it would stay out of her way during the training session. Dressed in a long sleeved T-shirt, breeches, and riding boots, she entered the barn at quarter to eight to the sounds of hooves rustling in the stalls as horses munched their morning hay.

The comfort of a horse barn had always been her sanctuary—until it wasn't.

Reyes stepped out of a stall on the far side of the aisle from Fire, making her heart rate speed up. Geez, was he the only one who worked here? She realized with his father gone, and only eight stalls occupied, the answer was likely *yes*.

He paused when he saw her, his expression slightly surprised as he glanced at his watch, but then his jaw set, and he continued forward.

Clearly he'd expected her to be late. She gave him a

tight smile and reached for the stall latch as he walked past. When her conscience got the better of her, she spoke over her shoulder while sliding the door open. "Thank you for taking my things to the house last night."

"All part of the job," he quipped.

His dry tone drew her head around, but he'd already disappeared into the office. So much for trying to be civil. She huffed out a breath and tried to put him out of her mind while getting Fire tacked up for work. Thankfully, he seemed closer to his regular self, nudging her shoulder as she tightened the saddle cinch. She took a moment to hug his head to her chest, placed a kiss on his forehead, and said a small prayer today went well.

Well would mean a decent trainer, successful jumps, and Reyes too busy here in the barn to be anywhere near the arena as a distraction.

After strapping her helmet on, she led Fire from the barn a couple minutes before eight. A glance around revealed no vehicle other than the hunk of junk Reyes had driven last night, and nobody waiting for her in the arena. Maybe her trainer should've received the, *"Don't be late,"* warning, too.

Raine shook off her frown as she led her gelding toward the mounting block. No big deal. She and Fire would start warm-up until they arrived.

"I'll give you a leg up."

Reyes' too-close voice made her jerk around with a gasp. How the heck had she not heard him walk up behind her? Only, he really was too close, and her helmet visor bumped right into his chest.

Damn, he smelled good. Like hay, and the outdoors, and an underlying hint of fresh citrus swirled in with all kinds of male goodness.

"Sorry." His hands grasped her shoulders to set her back a step.

She flicked her gaze up and just as quickly dropped it again while turning back to Fire. Those green eyes of his were way too damn pretty in the morning sunlight.

"I had it, but, yeah, whatever." His chest brushed against her shoulder as he bent to offer his interlocked hands for her boot. Two seconds later, she was in the saddle and looking down at him as she gathered the reins with shaky hands. "Thanks."

"Yep." He patted Fire's neck and headed for the arena fence.

Raine blew out a silent sigh, her stomach tightening at the thought of him watching them practice. Then she got a good look inside the arena and her annoyance spiked as she squeezed her knees to signal Fire forward. All the rails were on the ground. Not a single jump was set up with even an inch of air between the rail and the dirt.

"What is this?" she demanded once she'd ridden through the open gate.

"Back to basics," Reyes replied.

"This is ridiculous. I'm not some ten-year-old beginner." She twisted in her seat to glare at him as he joined her inside the arena. Then she swept her furious gaze toward the barn, and the driveway beyond. "And why is it *I'm* not supposed to be late, but this guy—or woman?—isn't even here yet?"

"Who says he isn't here yet?"

The fake innocent tone of his voice instantly stiffened her spine. The tension in her body sent Fire dancing sideways, and she spun him in a circle to settle him down before finally looking at Reyes. Amusement in his sunlit gaze made her stomach drop out from under her.

"*You?*"

He offered a slight smile with an affirmative tilt of his head. "Me."

"Why didn't you just say so last night?"

"And miss this fun?"

She suppressed the urge to scream, but still tossed out, "Asshole," before urging Fire into a trot around the outdoor arena. She needed a few rounds to cool off. Reyes didn't say a word as she passed the first time. Nor the second.

Smart man.

By the time he'd climbed the fence on her third round and perched on the top rail to watch, she'd managed to get her aggravation under control.

"Run the course," he instructed as she and Fire approached. "Mix it up, but take it easy. I want to get a feel for your rhythm."

"Our rhythm is fine," she retorted.

Still, she grit her teeth and did as he said. Three times through, during which he stayed silent. Her annoyance flared yet again. It was one thing to let her cool off, and Lord knew she didn't want to talk to the guy, but if he was supposed to be training her, he was going to have to say something at some point.

Finally, she rode over to the fence and planted Fire directly in front of him. "What exactly are your qualifications?"

He sat balanced on the top rail, hands braced on either side of him, the sun adding blond highlights to his brown hair. "I did some jumping back in high school."

When he didn't add more, she tilted her head in disbelief. "Are you serious right now?"

He smiled while sitting up straighter. "I did jump some in high school, though nowhere near your level. However, I have been training horses with my dad since I was fourteen. I took a six year break while in the military, but after coming home almost two years ago, I've been working solo."

Raine snorted. "With what, the few horses my aunt keeps here now?"

"You do know Janine rescues horses, right? Most of them off-the-track-thoroughbreds?"

"Of course." Her dad wrote a check every year to contribute to his sister-in-law's non-profit.

"Well, then you should know, she doesn't keep them all. We celebrated a hundred and fifty rehomed last month."

She had not known *that,* but she should've. It was an extremely impressive number.

"When they leave here," Reyes added, "they've been transitioned into new careers in jumping, hunting, dressage, trail riding, pleasure driving—whatever we discover best suits them."

Still irritated over the whole situation, she snipped, "So what…are you supposed to be a horse whisperer or something?"

He dropped his gaze as he lifted a shoulder. "The horses respond to me. Always have."

Like Fire in the trailer. "And how many riders have you worked with?"

"You would be the first."

"Perfect." Her dad was putting her Olympic hopes in the hands of a guy with no professional experience at all. "How could this go wrong?"

He lifted his gaze once more, long dark lashes shadowing his eyes. "I saw the tapes of your last two events. Whatever you were doing back home wasn't working. If you ask me, you've got nothing to lose."

"Well, I didn't ask you, did I?"

"Technically, you did."

"That was a rhetorical question. You do know what rhetorical means, don't you?"

He smirked at her sarcasm before jumping down from the fence to stride toward one of the jumps. She watched as he put the rails in the cups and then moved on to the next one.

Good. About damn time they got down to real work.

When the last rail was in place, he raised a hand over his head and swiveled his wrist in a circle to indicate she should get started. Despite wanting the real jumps, her nerves tingled to life as she urged Fire forward. Once around the arena to loosen him up, because her tension from the exchange with Reyes was making him antsy.

Way number one it would go wrong—the guy annoyed the hell out of her and made her nervous. Which made her horse nervous. Not a good combination.

Stop thinking about him.

Focus on Fire. Focus on the jumps.

Imagine walking into the Olympic stadium with the U.S. Equestrian Team, the American flag rippling in all its glory above your head.

Her dad had painted that picture with her so often over the years, the image sprang to life with ease.

Another half-round at an easy canter settled her and Fire into the familiar rhythm that had gotten them to the top, so she reined him onto the course. Over the next half-hour, Reyes directed them through a multitude of combinations. Other than the called out instructions, he simply watched. His intense scrutiny was really starting to mess with her head, especially when for the third time in a row, Fire refused an easy one meter vertical.

"You're breaking the rhythm," Reyes called out, shaking his head.

"*He* won't go over the jump."

"Because you're telling him not to."

"I am not."

"You're easing up on approach, sending mixed signals, and it's throwing him off. He doesn't know what you want him to do."

Just like Charlie, he was blaming her for Fire's refusal. Her jaw ached from the force of her clenched teeth. How did no one understand what the fall had done to him? He was afraid. It was going to take time for him to get over it and get his confidence back. She knew her horse better than they did, damn it.

"He needs a break," she announced. And so did she.

Before Reyes could disagree with her, she swung her leg over and dismounted. She didn't get more than two strides toward the gate when he moved into their path.

He held out his hand, palm up. "Give me the reins."

"I can take care of him myself."

"That's a given. But first I want to try something."

She wanted to tell him to go to hell, but after a long moment, she slapped the reins into his palm. He draped them back over Fire's neck while moving to the opposite side to lower the right stirrup. Grudgingly, she lowered the one on her side, too.

When he joined her on the left side, she wordlessly bent to offer her interlocked hands and boosted him up into the saddle. His western boots and jeans looked completely out of place with her English saddle, but his form was flawless as he nudged Fire into a trot, and then a canter. He made a circuit of the arena, to get a feel for the horse beneath him, she assumed, then took him over a couple of the jumps Fire had completed for her with ease.

Next, he pointed him toward the vertical Fire had refused three times in a row, and Raine's entire body went rigid. Her breath shortened as her pulse beat faster.

Fire sailed right over without a second of hesitation.

A flash of relief was replaced by fury. She clenched her fists at her sides as Reyes rode up and dismounted. Because she totally expected a smug smile, his solemn expression left her confused.

"And what do you think that proved?" she accused. "That you're better than me?"

"No. That you're the one who's afraid, not your horse."

Her stomach lurched as if she'd just done a loop-de-loop on a roller coaster immediately after lunch. She wanted to grab the reins from his hand and run, but she forced herself to face him squarely. "I am not afraid."

"There's no shame in it, Raine. That was a tough wreck by anyone's standards."

"How would you know?"

"I saw the tape."

Of course he had. Seemed he'd seen all kinds of tape lately. Her gut clenched at the thought of him watching her fail.

"It's going to take some working through," he

added. "Especially if you haven't even admitted it to yourself yet."

"There's nothing to admit," she bit out. "We're fine."

"Come on now. You don't believe that any more than I do."

The surprising gentleness in his tone made her eyes sting, and she snatched the reins to lead Fire back to the barn.

"I didn't say we were done," Reyes said behind her.

She ignored him and kept walking while reaching up to yank at the strap of her helmet. After pulling it off, she transferred it to her left hand with the reins so she could swat away the stray strands of hair tickling her cheeks.

"Hey."

All the gentle was gone from his voice. And the command that had taken its place pissed her off enough to yell over her shoulder, "*I* say we're done. In fact, I'm done with *all of this*." She reached back to wave her arm in a huge circle to indicate him and the entire arena behind her as she continued toward the barn. "I'm calling my dad, and I'm going home."

"Wow. You gave it what? Two hours?"

"That's all it took to see you don't have a clue what you're doing."

"So, you're not only afraid of the jumps, you're afraid of me, too."

His voice came from right behind her, and she

flinched before whirling around. "I'm not afraid of you. I just can't stand you."

Liar.

He crossed his arms. "Whatever you gotta tell yourself."

She practically growled as she leaned forward. "I *don't* like you. Sorry if it hurts your fragile little ego, but you were a jerk last summer, and you've been a jerk since I got here last night. The truth is, it's taking everything I have not to smack you right now."

His eyebrows shot up as he gave a short laugh of disbelief. "Really?"

"Yes, *really.*"

"Well, by all means then, go ahead." He bent closer, his green eyes locked with hers as he murmured softly, "I dare you."

She narrowed her gaze at the cocky taunt. When his lips twitched into a smirk, she lost it.

5

*R*eyes heard the *crack* as pain exploded in his cheek. His head snapped to the side, and he froze for a stunned moment. Slowly, he turned his head back to Raine. Fiery red bloomed in her cheeks—likely matching his left one.

"I can't believe you just did that."

Her chin lifted defensively as she took a wary step back. "You told me to."

"Yeah, but I didn't think you'd *actually* do it."

"Well, word to the wise—don't dare a Diamond, 'cuz we don't back down." With that parting shot, she pivoted and resumed her trek to the barn.

He raised his hand to his throbbing cheek as he followed at a distance. Hell, she was a lot stronger than she looked. Then again, he shouldn't be surprised when she spent her days in a saddle controlling a twelve-hundred pound beast. He'd underestimated her for sure

—yet another lesson learned at the hand of a Diamond in less than two days.

However, he had his answer, didn't he? Yes, she was afraid, but she wasn't willing to give up without a fight. Now all she needed to do was come to that realization by herself.

Reyes went to the office to do paperwork while Raine took care of her horse. A half an hour later, he heard her boots a moment before her slim form shadowed the doorway. He glanced up from an email on the computer from Janine about Morning Glory's adoption.

"I'm not leaving," Raine stated.

Strong and smart.

He gave her a mocking smile. "Daddy said you can't come home?"

Her jaw clenched, and her hands fisted at her sides. Man, it was so easy to push her buttons. He couldn't help but wonder how responsive she'd be if he pushed other buttons. More enjoyable buttons.

His blood warmed, and he had to swallow hard against a wave of want.

"I didn't call my dad."

He'd already figured that. Her father had been very adamant on the phone yesterday, and if she had called him, Reyes was pretty sure she wouldn't be all blustery and challenging right now. She'd decided to prove to herself—and him—she wasn't afraid of anything. He'd like to say *good*, but first he needed her to face what had happened. Only when she admitted her fear

47

could she confront it and *then* prove she could get past it.

In the meantime, a few more buttons couldn't hurt. "I'm proud of you, Princess. That's a big step all by yourself."

Her nose scrunched up in a scowl. If she knew how cute she looked, she'd be even more pissed than she was right now.

Defiance glittered in her eyes as she crossed her arms. "I'm only staying to watch you fail."

"Then we're both agreed." He leaned forward, bracing his forearms on the desk. "We'll be doing things my way."

"Whatever." She started to turn away, then paused to look back. "My dad must be paying you a lot to make this all worth it."

Reyes drew back the slightest bit, surprised not only by her words, but the offense they sparked. "He's not paying me a dime."

Her gaze narrowed, and she hesitated a beat. "He can afford it, you know."

"You can all afford it," he tossed back. "You're Diamonds."

She gave him a sugar-sweet smile. "You should've negotiated."

"Your uncle asked me to help. It never even crossed my mind to ask for anything above my regular wages."

"Hmm. Note to self. Save words to the wise for someone who's actually wise."

She was gone before he could tell her not everything was about money. Granted, he hadn't taken this assignment willingly, but even if he had, he wouldn't have expected to get paid more for doing something Mark and Janine already generously compensated him for. And if he was being honest, he wanted to help her get her confidence back so she could once more be the winner he'd seen in earlier tapes.

He glanced out the window to see Raine crossing the wide expanse of lawn to the guest house. He'd intended to schedule an afternoon session, but he didn't have her phone number—a fact he'd need to rectify—and he wasn't about to go chasing after her. Since it was only the first day, he decided tomorrow would be soon enough to set a firm schedule.

Returning his attention to the computer, he sent a message to Janine agreeing Moring Glory was ready to graduate, and yes, the Hamiltons would be a great fit for the mare. Then he confirmed a Friday morning showing with the couple who'd already adopted two horses from them.

As for the rest of today, he was going to take his unexpected afternoon off and get out for a ride. Yesterday's schedule had been thrown off after he'd been ambushed by Mark, and Taz was as anxious for some exercise as he was for some solitude on the trails.

Though, come to think of it, the heaviness that usually settled in his chest after a few days of being restrained to the barn was absent. In fact, there was an energy invigorating his body that had him looking forward to tomorrow morning when he should be dreading dealing with the headstrong brunette. But Raine provided a challenge—one he hadn't realized he'd even wanted until she announced she was staying.

"I'm only staying to watch you fail."

The memory of those words sparked a smirk. He was pretty sure she'd said that just to be contrary. It would make no sense for her to sabotage him on purpose, because if he failed, she failed. And he'd stake his job on that being the last thing she wanted.

For the rest of the morning and an hour after lunch, he took care of miscellaneous chores until it was time for a ride. In the middle of saddling his thoroughbred, his older brother strode into the barn. "Hey, Rey. You heading out or finishing up?"

He glanced at Dev over the saddle. "Heading out. Want to come?"

"Hell yeah. Who you got for me?"

"Morning Glory or Stimpy. Both could use the exercise."

"No offense to Morning Glory, but Stimpy's my guy."

Dev headed to the tack room for a saddle and bridle, and Reyes noted his limp was almost undetectable today. It became more pronounced in damp weather, but even so, his brother had progressed in all areas since January. Thanks to time and therapy—and Shelby.

It had seemed strange at first, Dev with the

youngest of the Diamonds, but she'd been a key part of bringing him back to the man he used to be. Of making him realize he still had a whole hell of a lot to offer the world outside of the military. Their whole family had loved her before, but now, they'd be forever grateful.

"Shelby working at the clinic?" he asked as they rode out side by side a few minutes later. She'd had the grand opening of her veterinary clinic for low-income families a couple of weeks ago. And Dev had set up a self-defense and tactical training gym right next door.

"She's at the guest house visiting her cousin, so I decided to tag along."

"Ah. Should've guessed that."

Dev shot him a sideways look that held a combination wince and grin. "I hear you're her new trainer."

He laughed as he worked at containing Taz's energy beneath him. "If that came from Raine, I imagine you heard quite the earful."

"She's not a fan," his brother confirmed with a chuckle. "Shelby sang your praises, but Raine was having none of that."

Reyes shrugged. "My job is to get her back to competition level in her jumping, not gain a groupie."

"A groupie?" Dev scoffed. "You fancy yourself a rock star?"

"I was sticking with the 'fan' analogy, that's all." He made the turn for the trail leading into the forest, and his brother reined Stimpy to follow.

"Shelby was telling me on the drive over about Raine's accident last year."

"Yeah." He slowed Taz until they were riding side by side again. The afternoon sunlight slanted through the trees, throwing dappled shade over them and the horses. "As far as I know, she hasn't been over the jump she wrecked on since the accident. She insists she and her horse are fine, but I saw it this morning—she's scared spitless when they head for that jump."

"And you're going to fix it?"

"I'm going to try."

"I wasn't aware you were working with horses *and* riders now."

"I'm doing a favor for Mark."

Like Dev had also done a favor for the senator when he'd agreed to be Shelby's bodyguard back in February.

After a moment of silence, his brother glanced over. "You know what it sounds like?"

His solemn, sympathetic tone had Reyes nodding. Neither one of them needed to say post traumatic stress out loud. They both dealt with their own demons enough to recognize someone else's.

"Has she talked to a professional yet?"

"I didn't ask, but I doubt it." She couldn't even admit her fear, so yeah, he highly doubted she'd gone to therapy for it.

"And how about you?"

"I'm good." He felt his brother's intense gaze and

shot him a quick glance while insisting, "Really, I've been feeling much better."

"I didn't ask if you were good, I asked if you've talked to anyone yet."

"I'm talking to you." At his brother's rough sigh, he met his gaze. "Listen, man, I'm living my therapy. Working with the horses. Finding them homes with Janine. Riding out here in the woods. It's been helping more than you know." And it was mostly true.

"You still sleeping with the lights on?"

Reyes tensed, and Taz gave a little lurch forward. He tightened his grip on the reins and brought the thoroughbred back to a walk.

"I'll take that as a *yes,*" Dev said dryly.

He shrugged, but remained silent. Talking to his brother helped sometimes, and other times, not so much. It left him feeling like a fraud. So what if he had trouble sleeping if it was completely dark? Big whoop if he spent a buck or two more in electricity each month. It wasn't like he'd nearly lost his leg like Dev. Or lost his life like Cory Neider the day the bomb had exploded.

The little flicker of resentment that accompanied those thoughts was immediately squashed. While he knew PTSD didn't have to be extreme to be legitimate, and everyone's threshold was different, he also wasn't going to wallow in self-pity when his physical issues had resolved themselves, and his only visible reminder was a thin white scar mostly hidden by the goatee he kept neatly trimmed. He hadn't been left with years of recovery and endless hours of physical therapy like so many others.

At times he almost wished he had been.

Almost.

Dev reined Stimpy closer, gaining his attention. "So, what's your plan with Raine?"

He never thought he'd see the day, but Reyes welcomed the return subject of his new challenge so he could focus on the therapy of the ride.

To answer his brother's question, he said, "First I've got to get her to talk. Then I'm going to get her over that jump."

6

"It's still a little unreal to see you and Dev together." Raine handed Shelby a bottle of iced tea as they stepped out onto the guest house patio. "I'm really happy for you."

"Thanks." She twisted the cap off her drink. "Sometimes I still can't believe it myself."

"Well, you guys seem great together."

"We are. Don't get me wrong, it was bumpy at first, but now things are really good."

Shelby's soft smile was so sappy, Raine's chest thumped with envy. She smiled as her cousin kicked off her sandals and sat on the edge of the pool. Having changed into a lycra sport tank and yoga capris for her workout, she dropped down beside her, facing the mountains as they swished their feet in the warm water.

"Remember that summer we were fifteen, and we spent the day at the pool with everyone up by the main house when he was home on leave? We were a couple of giggling idiots."

Shelby laughed. "Oh my God, I know. But then again, who could blame us? The Torrez brothers were as hot then as they are now."

Ignoring the plural, she gave a dramatic sigh. "No more drooling over Dev for me."

Shelby snorted and leaned to nudge her with her shoulder. "You don't fool me, Cuz."

"What?"

"Don't *what* me. You played it cool, but we both know you were teasing the shit out of Reyes back then."

Yeah, she'd gone in and out of the house for more lemonade than she could possibly drink. And each time, she made sure her path inside was right past his chair, or wherever he was in the pool. She'd been loud and outgoing while playing volleyball and chicken with her cousins, but the problem was, no matter how much attention she tried to draw to herself, he'd openly ignored her. Same as last July.

"I didn't even talk to him," she protested.

"But you made sure he couldn't take his eyes off you."

She rolled her eyes, though her pulse skipped at that revelation. She hadn't known he'd noticed her. "Reyes has always had a chip on his shoulder with me. Last summer we ran into each other down at the stables and he was a jerk. He's still a jerk."

Except for the luggage.

56

She shoved aside the flicker of guilt for purposely overlooking that when she called him a jerk to his face earlier. Why should she feel bad when she'd tried to thank him, only to have him brush her gratitude aside with his flippant comeback about it being part of his job? It so wasn't.

Shelby frowned beside her. "That's so weird. And so unlike Reyes."

"Lucky me," she quipped before changing the subject. "How's everything going now that your clinic is open? Must Love Paws is an awesome name."

"That was all Honor, and yeah, everyone loved the name. And things are going really good so far. The community seems really happy to have us."

"That's cool."

"You should come check it out while you're here," Shelby suggested.

"I'd love to. On a slightly different note, do you all still do brunch even when Uncle Mark and Aunt Janine are in Washington? Because I'm having dinner with Grandpa and Grandma tonight, but I want to see everyone—especially the babies."

"Oh, my God, they're the best," Shelby gushed with a huge grin. "I *love* being an aunt."

"I bet. None of my brothers are even close to getting married," she pouted.

"I'll share, and yes, we still do brunch. Wait until you see the babies. Maverick has caught up on every-

57

thing after being nearly two months early, and Ava is so precious."

Maverick was Merit and Mae's little boy, born last November. Ava belonged to Asher and Honor, and had been born in January.

Raine wasn't sure she could stand to wait until Sunday even if it was only three days away. "What about Celia and Robert? Any talk from them about kids?"

"They're trying, but no luck yet." Her cousin made a sad face. "I pray it happens soon for them, though, because I know Loyal and Rox are already trying."

She wasn't surprised. They'd been talking about kids at their wedding back in February.

"Does it give you the bug?" Raine teased.

Shelby's grin answered before her words. "A little, but we'd like some time to ourselves after the wedding. Especially after how crazy everything was this past spring."

Crazy was an understatement to describe what Bells and Dev had gone through with her psycho stalker. She reached out to squeeze her cousin's hand. "I'm so glad you're okay after all of that."

"Thanks. I was lucky to have Dev—even though I didn't want him as a bodyguard at first."

"Good thing he was."

"Believe me, I know." She fiddled with her bottle cap before offering a sideways smile. "And on that note…I wanted to say, make sure you give Reyes a chance, okay?"

Her pulse skipped, because her first thought after their talk of marriage and babies was, *give him a chance with what?* But there was only one thing her cousin was talking about. "Dad didn't give me much of a choice. And unfortunately, he's right. I'm getting nowhere with Charlie right now."

"Rey is really good with horses, Raine. And when I say really good, I mean crazy amazing."

"Yeah, but no experience training riders at all." Resentment bled into her voice. She couldn't believe her dad would put her future in his hands.

"Maybe he'll be just what you and Fire need," Shelby said.

Raine gave her cousin a brief smile. "I guess we'll see, won't we?"

Except she knew, she didn't *need* anything, least all him.

The next morning, Raine kept her gaze trained straight ahead as she passed the stable office on her way to Fire's stall.

"Hey—hold up. Can you come in here for a minute?"

Reyes' loud voice made her pulse skip a few beats

before taking off like a thoroughbred from the starting gate. Having already been fighting a bit of irritating breathlessness from the thought of seeing him again this morning, she halted, closed her eyes to suck in a fortifying breath, then blew it back out again before backtracking.

She had whole month of having to see him every day, so might as well get used to it, right?

Right.

Only, one look at the man and any calming effects flew out the barn doors. Yesterday, he'd worn a thin button up over his T-shirt, with the sleeves rolled up, tanned forearms on full display. Today was already warmer than yesterday, and she got the full treat of not only sexy, muscled forearms, but defined biceps stretching the short sleeves of a dark green T-shirt.

She dragged her gaze up from his drool-worthy arms. Damn it all. With his golden-tipped, caramely hair and those long, dark lashes, he was way too attractive for her peace of mind.

When she realized he was giving her a once-over, too, her pulse stumbled again, and her nipples instantly tightened. She crossed her arms to hide the reaction. His lashes lifted at the movement, and heat infused her cheeks as their gazes connected.

"What?" she asked, the word coming out clipped and defensive.

He gestured to a straight-back chair in front of the desk. "I set up a schedule for your training. I figured we should both know what's going on."

He set up the schedule, because *he* figured. She dropped down onto the seat, arms still crossed. "Yeah. *We* both should."

He flicked his gaze up to hers as he handed a sheet of paper across the desk. Raine focused on the paper, snatching it from him to scan the agenda line by line. He should've *figured* she should get a say in her own schedule.

A flick of her wrist sent the paper sliding back across the desk. "This isn't going to work."

His gaze narrowed as he leaned forward on his forearms. She glanced down, then forced her attention back to his face.

"What's wrong with it?" he asked.

"For starters, you didn't even bother to ask me what might work for me."

"I told you yesterday, we're doing this my way."

"It's *my* career," she snapped.

"And it's *my* job to get you back where you need to be," he countered. "Except it's only *part* of my job."

She had to consciously unclench her jaw, though she didn't speak. After a long moment, he sat back, the leather office chair creaking with his movements.

"What's wrong with the schedule?" he repeated, his tone unexpectedly softer.

"The only time you've left for my workouts is in the middle of the day, and it's not even enough time."

"You're worried about working out?" he asked with a frown.

"Yes." She drew the word out on purpose. "If you had bothered to ask, or you know, ever worked with a professional rider, you'd know strength training and cardio is just as important as the riding."

His frown deepened as he reached for the schedule. "You can't fit it in before or after?"

"If I do my usual three hours in the morning, I'll have to get up at four-thirty. If I do it after, my day won't end until after seven o'clock. It's a part of my job, and it needs to be part of my schedule, not something I fit in after hours."

"Fine. I'll move the afternoon riding session back an hour and a half. Then you can fit it in either before or after lunch."

"I always ride in the mornings and workout in the afternoon. Then I only have to shower once."

Shower? Did she really have to say the word *shower* to him? In the next moment, she imagined him standing in a cloud of steam, biceps bulging on his raised arms as hot water chased suds down the length of his long, lean body. Her cheeks burned at the alarmingly vivid image just as his gaze flicked up to hers.

Oh my God, imagine if he could read my mind!

He cleared his throat and returned his attention to the paper. "You ran the other morning," he stated, his voice slightly rough.

"That was an exception because of being cooped up in the truck the day before. It's not the norm."

He nodded and shrugged at the same time. "Regardless, I have a specific reason for morning and afternoon sessions,"

"And as I just told you, *I* have a specific reason for getting all the riding done in the morning."

His mouth pressed into a grim line before he set the paper down, leaned his forearms on the desk again, and linked his fingers together over the top of it. "Then let's compromise."

"There's nothing to compromise."

"Sure there is. We'll do my schedule Monday, Wednesday, and Friday, and yours on Tuesday, Thursday, and Saturday."

Though she knew it was childish, the thought of giving in even partially irked her to no end. Back home, Charlie never had a problem following the schedule she set up. Same with every other trainer she'd had, because they worked for her, not the other way around.

Except Reyes didn't work for her or her dad, and clearly, he wasn't about to be bossed around.

He blew out a breath that sounded as frustrated as she felt. "We've got twenty-nine days to go here, Raine. It'll go a lot faster if we work together."

The words were an unexpected slap in the face. He was already counting down the days.

She couldn't blame him. She wanted time to pass faster, too. Yet, hearing him voice the desire outright made her chest tighten with resentment—and another emotion she refused to acknowledge.

"Unless your plan is to purposely sabotage this

whole thing," he added. "Seeing as you only stayed to watch me fail."

She rolled her eyes. "I didn't really mean that."

"Good. Because that would be really stupid on your part."

Completely annoyed at the inference, she shoved to her feet and reached for the paper and pen near his fore-arm. Her fingers brushed against his warm skin for a brief second, and she jerked back from the contact at the same time he moved his arm. Ignoring the hot, electric tingles spreading through her body, she leaned over to write down her version of the schedule for the days he'd designated at hers.

"There. All set." She slapped the pen down and straightened. "And today is Thursday, just so you know."

"I'm well aware of what day it is."

"Good. Then I'll meet you in the arena in fifteen."

She turned to leave, quick strides carrying her to the door.

"Raine."

His tone was firm, yet it also held an unexpected plea that had her pausing in the doorway.

"I was a squad leader in the Army. My orders were followed without question. That's how we got things done."

"Yeah, well, I am not one of your soldiers," she snipped.

"No, you most definitely are not," he muttered.

A quick twist caught him jerking his gaze up from her ass. She was surprised by a slight tinge of pink in his cheeks as he straightened in the chair.

"Anyway," he said quickly. "I apologize for not talking to you about the schedule first. It won't happen again."

She nodded and left, because she didn't know what to say when he went and said something nice. After telling her yesterday they'd be doing things his way, the apology was right up there with the luggage.

$\mathcal{R}$eyes crossed the lawn toward the guest house later Thursday evening. He'd debated this move for most of the afternoon, but thinking back over Raine's morning riding session, he knew he needed to get through to her sooner than later.

Halfway through the session, he'd put her on Taz. Or tried to. She'd gotten pissed off and left early— because she knew if she got up on his horse and still didn't make it over the jump, he'd know for sure it was her who kept refusing, not Diamond Fire. He already knew for sure, and none of her blustery, logical excuses changed his mind.

Coming up on the side of the house, he angled toward the front until a splash from the back patio made him pause. Doing his best to block the immediate memory of a little red bikini, he switched direction.

Landscape lighting lit the way around back, where the in-ground pool glowed an inviting Caribbean blue in the dark night.

Clad in a black one-piece, Raine's slim form cut sinuously through the water, her movements sure and swift as she swam from one end of the pool to the other. He watched for a moment, wondering if a nighttime swim was part of her daily workout, or if she was driven by something else. A need to be completely exhausted just so she could catch a few hours of sleep before the dreams woke her up?

Stop projecting.

He moved to the edge of the pool, lining up with her before taking a knee to swish his hand in the water to get her attention.

Her fingers brushed against his when she reached for the wall. She simultaneously jerked to the side and shoved away, the move sending a wave rolling across the pool. Surfacing with a sputter, she ripped off her swim goggles and glared up at him.

"Damn it, Reyes, you scared the hell out of me!"

He pushed back into a squat. "I wasn't sure how long it would take for you to realize I was here, and I didn't want to be all creepy by just standing and watching."

"Yeah, well, you failed."

When he grinned at her disgruntled tone, her glare intensified.

She swiped a hand across her face, brushing aside the wet strands of hair that had escaped her long braid. "What do you want?"

"To talk."

She huffed and rolled her eyes. "If this is about earlier, I'll make up the time tomorrow."

"It's not about earlier."

"Then what could you possibly want to talk about?"

"Your accident."

Her head jerked up. Panic flashed a second before her expression shuttered, and she averted her gaze with a shake of her head. "Nope."

"I'm not leaving until we talk, Raine."

"Gonna be a long night for you then."

Before he could say anything more, she put the goggles back on and swirled around to resume swimming. Reyes blew out a loud sigh as he rose from his squat. Raine reached the far end, executed a rapid turn underwater, and swam back toward him. At his end of the pool, she flipped and started another lap without slowing down.

The way she attacked the water confirmed she was doing her damnedest to out swim her demons. Problem was, his mind was starting to wander off task. Instead of considering how to get her to open up about the accident, he was thinking about his hands gliding over her pale skin instead of the water.

Or better yet, his lips.

You're here to train her, not maul her.

Right. Stay on task.

Except she was right. If he waited for her to give in, he'd probably end up sleeping out here in one of the deck chairs.

Fuck that.

Reaching up behind his head, he grabbed a fistful of T-shirt to drag it over his head. He bent to pull off one boot, then the other, then stripped off his jeans and socks. When he was down to his boxer briefs, he dove into the water and swam after her. The temperature was warm enough to not be a shock, but cool enough to be refreshing.

Raine did that underwater somersault turn, saw him, and jackknifed to the surface. He rose up from his dive a few feet from her. She'd pulled off the goggles again and was already yelling.

"—kidding me right now? What the hell?"

He treaded water while reaching with both hands to rake his dripping hair off his forehead. "I told you we need to talk, and I don't have all night to wait you out."

"That's your problem, not mine."

Her words were full of bravado, but her expression had a frantic edge as she moved to swim away.

Reyes lunged to catch her arm. Combined momentum made their bodies collide under the water. Shock widened her eyes, and a gasp parted her lips at the same time a molten wave of awareness flooded his veins. Heart thudding hard, he released her and eased back a couple feet. She was already feeling threatened, last thing he wanted was for her to be afraid of him physically.

But she remained facing him instead of rushing to get away again. A glimpse of her pink tongue swiping across her glistening lips had him biting back a low groan.

Raising his gaze to the spiked lashes framing her luminous hazel eyes, he forced his brain to stop thinking with his dick. "Do you even want to compete anymore?"

Surprise flashed across her face a second before her forehead furrowed while she averted her gaze. "Of course I do. I just don't understand why you want to make me talk about what happened. I've been trying to forget it."

"*That's* why. You need to face it, not forget it." When she gave a wild shake of her head, he leaned to the side and scissored his legs to move back into her line of vision. "Trust me. I know what I'm talking about."

"You saw the tape, but you weren't there."

"I'm talking in general. We all have our demons to fight."

Her angry gaze speared into his. "Oh really? And what's your demon?"

"I don't like the dark." The words slipped out without thought, and his breath seized in his throat as she gaped at him in surprise.

What the fuck? Where had that come from?

"Why don't you like the dark?"

His heart beat thunderously loud in his ears. "This isn't about me."

She tilted her head. "Not so fun when the tables are turned, is it?"

Definitely not. Time to turn them back. "You said Diamonds don't back down. It's time to face this head on."

Annoyance narrowed her gaze. "Is that supposed to be a dare or something?"

He arched his brows and shrugged. "If that's what it takes."

She gave a slow shake of her head, then twisted around to swim toward the deepest, darkest corner of the pool. Her movements were slow and measured instead of a frantic escape. Reyes followed, keeping a good two feet between them when she folded her arms on the edge and stared into the privacy hedges along the back side of the patio.

After a moment of silence, she said softly, "How about we compromise?"

Her soft, almost empathetic tone made his gut clench with foreboding. He hadn't turned the tables far enough. Resting one arm on the brick rim, he warily studied her shadowed profile. "There's nothing to compromise."

She turned her head to meet his gaze. "Tell me why

you don't like the dark, and I'll tell you about the accident."

Fuck.

He'd given her a hand grenade, and she'd just pulled the pin.

8

$\mathcal{R}$aine saw the hunted look in Reyes' eyes and knew exactly how he felt. What she hadn't expected though, was the guilt that squeezed her chest when she watched his silent struggle with her negotiation.

It was only fair, and yet she had to bite her tongue to keep from telling him to forget it. She also had to lock each hand around the opposite wrist to keep from turning to him, from reaching out to touch his arm, his chest, or from wrapping her arms around his neck as she plastered her mouth and body to his. Bet he'd forget about talking then.

But as much as she wanted that, she also didn't. Because while the man could rile her up like no one else, little glimpses of decency, kindness, and compassion beneath his rough exterior had her dying to learn more about *that* guy.

Like why *he* was afraid of the dark.

He hadn't quite admitted that, but she could read between the lines. Same as he could apparently read between all of hers.

So she waited, her gaze memorizing the details of his face as he wrestled with his demons. Prominent eyebrows, high cheekbones, somewhat square jaw. She'd never been attracted to a guy with facial hair before, but his was neatly trimmed and a hell of a lot sexier than she ever would've expected.

Her attention snagged on a thin, pale scar along the edge of his whiskers on the right side of his chin. Illuminated by the underwater pool lights, it stood out in stark contrast to the darker tone of his skin.

That right there. She wanted to know how he got it, and when?

Did he have more scars? Where?

She wanted to draw along the white line with her fingertip. Lean forward and trace it with the tip of her tongue.

A wave of heat relaxed her grip on her arms. She started to turn the rest of her body toward him, until his lashes rose, and the torment in his darkened gaze froze her on the spot.

"Three years ago, I was blind for five days."

Of all the things he could've said, she never would've guessed something like that.

Three years ago…he'd been in the military then, hadn't he?

"It was one hundred percent. No shadows. Nothing."

Raine swallowed past a sudden lump in her throat and whispered, "What happened?"

"Bomb."

She waited for more, but he shook his head, his jaw set.

Raine sighed softly. Even without knowing details, she couldn't imagine how terrifying it must've been to be blinded and believe you'd never see again. And though it appeared his vision had recovered, after something like that, she could totally understand why he wouldn't like the dark.

Guilt crowded in again, and she reached out to cover his hand with hers. "I'm sorry."

His gaze shifted from her face to their hands. Self-conscious, she started to pull back, but he twisted his wrist and caught her fingers. "You have nothing to be sorry for—but it *is* your turn."

Her heart lurched in her chest both from the warmth of his touch and the insistence in his gruff voice. Her experience paled by comparison.

"My fall over a horse jump doesn't really seem like a big deal now, does it?"

"Don't do that." He shook his head, his fingers squeezing hers, the pressure almost painful before he relaxed his hold. "Never minimize what happened to you, Raine. It doesn't have to compare to what anyone else has gone through. Someone else's experience does not make the trauma you experienced any less worthy of serious attention."

The lump in her throat doubled in size, and she blinked against the painful sting of tears. She hadn't ever really thought of her accident as trauma. Pulling her hand free from his, she turned back to the hedges, wishing she could hide deep in the shadows of their branches. He didn't like the dark. She welcomed the cover it provided.

"The whole thing is still so vivid in my mind," she whispered. "Just thinking about it puts me right back in the moment."

Water lapped against her back when he moved closer. Close enough for her shoulder to brush against his chest, her hip against his thigh. The contact was like an anchor she didn't even know she needed.

"Fire was on point that day. He sailed over every jump without a single fault. We were well under the course time limit, and when we made the final turn, there were only three jumps left." She closed her eyes, and the image was *right there*.

With a quick shake of her head, she opened her eyes again.

But the jump remained.

"The way they were set up, I misjudged the height on the vertical, which was stupid, because I *knew* the height from the walk-through. But the visual between the rails threw me off and I timed it wrong. Fire tried to refuse at the last second, and I wouldn't let him, so he tried to clear it but got tangled in the rails—"

"Breathe," Reyes murmured next to her ear.

She sucked in a gasping breath and realized her whole body was shaking.

Against him.

When had he moved that close? When had he put his arm around her? And damn it, she was crying.

"Now let it back out."

He meant the breath, not her tears. She did as instructed while his hand rubbed up and down the arm not pressed against his chest.

"Take another."

The soothing tone of his voice calmed her enough to think past the panic. Except when her words replayed in her head, a sob escaped her tight lungs. "Oh my God—it was my fault."

"It's no one's fault."

"It was mine," she insisted with a shake of her head. "*I* messed up. Fire could've broken a leg—or both. I could've killed him."

"Is that why you're afraid of the jump?"

Raine gave a jerky nod without even thinking. "He trusted me. I forced him to jump, and he trusted me, and I could've killed him."

"He still trusts you."

"He shouldn't."

When Reyes pulled her closer, she didn't resist. Not

77

only did she not resist, she turned to wrap both arms around his neck and held on for dear life while he held them afloat with a one-handed grip on the edge. The pool was heated, but it was the warmth from his body that battled the chill of her memories as his lips brushed against her temple.

"He trusts you because you're his partner," he murmured. "You have to learn to trust yourself again. And to trust him, too."

That lump materialized in her throat once more. "I-I don't know if I can."

"That's why you're here," he said. "We're gonna figure this out, Raine. I promise."

She wished his words offered comfort, but she worried what they were going to figure out was equally as frightening as the jump. It brought the question he'd asked earlier back to the forefront. Did she want to compete anymore? Was she willing to risk so much for her dream of Olympic gold?

Was it *her* dream?

That question jolted hard, but just then, another press of Reyes' lips suddenly shifted her awareness.

Or maybe she was desperate for a diversion, mentally running from the uncertainty of her future.

Whatever the reason, she became conscious of every inch where their bodies touched. He held onto the side of the pool with one hand, his arm wrapped around her waist and hers around his neck. There wasn't an inch to separate them, from their hips, to where her breasts pressed against his bare chest.

She stilled, a hairsbreadth away from burying her face in the crook of his neck to drown herself in his arousing scent. When her brain registered his growing erection against her stomach, her pulse went all haywire. Molten heat flooded her veins before pooling into a yearning throb deep inside. Her nipples tightened, and her legs grew heavy from the wave of desire.

His breathing had become as shallow as hers. "Raine."

There was the tiniest note of regret in his voice. Or maybe a warning?

She ignored both. With her heart thumping like mad, she loosened her hold around his neck and flattened one palm against the side of his head to turn his face to hers. He didn't resist, but when her mouth found his, he tensed for a heart-stopping second.

With the proof of his desire against her belly, she licked at the seam of his lips, demanding his participation. From one breath to the next, his arm tightened around her ribs, and he slanted his mouth over hers to take control of the kiss with a toe-curling growl. His tongue dueled with hers, each stroke making the pulse deep in her core throb harder.

God, how many times had she thought of a moment like this over the past ten months—and even a few times before that? Reality was *so* much better than her imagination.

Swept up in a swirl of sensation and desire, she raised one leg to hook over his hip and ground herself against his hardness. Reyes sucked in a breath and muttered something against her lips, but dove right back in when she lifted her other leg and wrapped them both around his waist. How easy it would be to slip off her one-piece and his briefs and forget everything for a while.

Hopefully a long while.

The thought curved her lips under his, until his hand closed over her breast. Her breath hitched when he rubbed a thumb over her hard nipple, then she gasped when he pinched. She arched into his palm before maneuvering to drag one strap of her suit off her shoulder, then the other.

His gaze dropped as she peeled her suit down to her waist while lifting up so her breasts were out of the water for him to see and touch. She yearned for his hands on her again. His mouth. His tongue.

When she lifted higher in clear offering, the move earned her another low groan, but the unmistakable tone of regret in the rumbling sound sparked a flutter of panic in her chest.

"Fuck," he muttered while closing his eyes.

Yep. There it was again.

Her stomach sank, and she dunked herself back down until the water lapped at her chin. Still, her legs were locked around his waist. His erection still pressed against her core.

Dread chipped at her confidence as she asked, "What?"

He winced, his eyes still closed. "I can't."

She frowned in confusion, especially given his obvious arousal—until the word *bomb* echoed in her mind. Oh, God. Her heart thudded hard in dismay. Now she felt bad that he was all worked up and couldn't do anything about it.

"Reyes...I...I'm sorry."

His eyes popped open, and his forehead furrowed. "Don't apologize. It's my fault, not yours. I shouldn't have taken advantage."

Wait—*what?*

Confusion kept her from resisting as he pulled her suit back up to cover her chest, then gently unlocked her legs, and guided her hand to hang on to the edge of the pool instead of his shoulder.

As he pushed away from the edge to put distance between them, she said, "I'm confused. You said you can't."

"I work for your uncle."

What? "What does that have to do with what happened to you?"

The lines in his forehead cut deeper. "What do you mean, what happened to me?"

She bit the corner of her lip, not wanting to say it, but forcing it out anyway. Gently. Softly. Her voice full of sympathetic understanding. "The bomb?"

"The bomb? What does that—" His eyes went wide and shocked horror flashed across his face. "Oh, God, that is *not* what I meant when I said I can't."

"Then what did you mean?"

"Your uncle pays my salary."

It took a moment, but finally she made the connection. And was immediately pissed off. "So?"

"So, he asked me to help you, not sleep with you."

"Aren't you allowed to do what you want in your free time?"

His expression darkened. "That's not the point."

"Well, it's not like you're getting paid extra for me."

"Yet, he'd still probably fire me if he found out about this."

She narrowed her gaze, then shoved away from the wall. "Believe me, *I* won't be telling anyone," she advised over her shoulder.

He swam after her as she headed for the shallow end. "You're seriously mad right now?"

More like mortified.

"Gimmie a break here." He followed her up the steps. "I'm trying to do the right thing."

"The right thing would've been to not make me think you wanted this in the first place."

"I do want this, but you have to understand, I—"

"I understand perfectly." She grabbed her towel to wrap it around herself sarong style. Trying to salvage a smidgeon of her dignity, she half-turned toward him but didn't look at his face as she said stiffly, "I'm sorry I put you in a bad position. It won't happen again."

She spun for the patio doors, but didn't even make it one step before he gripped her arm and swung her back to face him. With her head tipped back to see his face, her breath caught when she saw the turmoil in his darkened green eyes.

"I want you, Raine. More than I've ever wanted anyone before." His lashes lowered, hiding all that heart-wrenching emotion. "But I *need* this job. *Because* of what happened, I need to be here, doing what I do."

His voice turned to pure gravel at the end, and her chest squeezed so tight she could barely breathe. She wanted to reach out and hug him, but he was still in only his wet, skin-tight boxer briefs, leaving nothing much to the imagination. Not to mention, if she pressed up against his bare chest again, there was no telling what she might do.

It took major effort to step back from temptation. As she moved back, his fingers skimmed down the back of her arm, past her elbow, and along the underside of her wrist before he finally dropped his arm to his side. As if he knew he had to let her go, but didn't want to.

She hugged her arms across her chest while suppressing a shiver. "I guess I'll see you in the morning then."

He gave a tight nod. "I have an adoption appointment for Morning Glory at eight, so you don't have to be down to the barn until nine."

"Nine it is." This time he didn't stop her when she forced her feet to take her inside.

Raine locked up, took a shower, and went to bed. She turned off the bedroom television at midnight.

When she got sick of staring at the ceiling round about two a.m., she went to the kitchen for a glass of water. As the cool liquid slid down her throat, her gaze was drawn across the sprawling lawn, toward the stables. The windows of the upstairs apartment were lit up as if it were evening instead of middle of the night.

Did Reyes leave the lights on to ward off the dark, or was he wide awake like her, wishing for what could have been?

$\mathcal{R}$eyes greeted Bob and Nancy Hamilton outside the barn precisely at eight the next morning before accompanying them inside. They would be the perfect distraction to keep his mind off facing Raine at nine.

His step faltered when he saw her standing outside Morning Glory's stall.

He'd barely slept after walking away from her last night. All he could think about when he closed his eyes was the feel of her lips beneath his, the seductive slide of her tongue, the weight of her breast in his palm, and the erotic sight of her tight nipples as the water lapped at her bare chest. Taking the edge off in the shower hadn't been nearly satisfying enough and only lasted for so long.

Even now, the quick, hesitant smile she shot him before introducing herself to the Hamiltons had his body taking notice. Christ, you'd think he was a horny teenager instead of a grown man perfectly capable of controlling his base urges. But another under-the-lashes glance from Raine had him clenching his jaw.

It was going to be a long day.

Damn—try a long three and a half weeks!

"I saw what happened at the end of the season," Nancy said, having recognized Raine's name from the jumping circuit. "That was a tough break. How is everything going?"

She grimaced at the older woman. "A little more down than up, but we're working hard to get back to where we were. Reyes is working with us for the next few weeks."

The openness of her reply surprised him. That was a step up from her usual, *"We're fine."*

"You're in good hands," Bob assured her before turning to Reyes. "We couldn't be happier with Ivy Rose and Dozer."

He seized the opportunity to shift focus. "Then you're going to be thrilled with Morning Glory. She reminded me of Dozer from the moment she arrived."

"Janice has told me all about her," Nancy said. "I've been looking forward to meeting her."

"Please, go ahead." He gestured toward the stall. "You know the drill by now, and if you have any questions, just ask."

The two of them moved ahead, and Raine sidled up beside him to ask in a low voice, "What's the drill?"

Acutely aware she was close enough for him to smell her fresh, flowery body wash, he kept his gaze focused on the mare. "They'll get her tacked up and head out to the arena for a bit before taking her out on the trails to see how she handles everything. If all goes well, we'll sign the papers, and she'll be off to her new home."

"How long have you been working with her?"

"About three months."

"And you've done this with over a hundred and fifty horses?"

The awe in her voice made his chest swell with pride. "I haven't worked with *all* of them, but I've had my fair share."

"Don't you get attached to the ones you work with?"

Unfortunately, yeah. And he was discovering it wasn't limited to the horses. The thought brought a frown as he replied, "It helps knowing they're going to a good home."

And that he helped them get there, which was exactly what he needed to do with Raine. Help her, and send her on her way.

Without touching her again.

Her fingers grazed his bicep, and he flinched.

When he shifted away while glancing down at her, she tilted her head with a frown of her own. "Is everything okay?"

"Yep," he said shortly.

"I was curious about how the adoptions worked,

87

that's why I came down early. But if it's a problem, I can come back at nine."

It wasn't her fault he couldn't think straight for wanting to take her upstairs, strip her bare, and bury himself deep inside her. Well, it was, but it wasn't.

"Don't be ridiculous," he bit out more harshly than he'd intended as he watched Bob and Nancy working with Morning Glory. "It's fine."

"Good." Raine crossed her arms, twisting on her heel to stare right at him with challenge written all over her face. He avoided her gaze, only to find his attention on the swell of her breasts as her crossed arms pushed them up in her snug T-shirt.

Fuck.

"And since I'm here," she continued, "Is there anything I can do to help?"

Reyes swallowed hard. *Yeah, you can*— "Muck the stalls."

Her eyebrows rose. "What?"

The affronted tone gave him the courage to finally look her in the eye. If he got her good and pissed her off, maybe she'd keep her distance. He'd put the horses out to pasture just before the Hamiltons arrived, and had planned to do chores between her morning and afternoon sessions, but this would work, too.

"You heard me." He cocked an eyebrow. "Unless you think you're too good to shovel shit?"

Her gaze narrowed. "I can muck a stall, Reyes."

"Good. Then do it." He abruptly turned and strode

toward the office before he gave in to the insane urge to pull her into his arms and kiss her breathless at eight a.m. in the morning.

An hour later, Morning Glory was in the trailer and on the way to her new home, and all the stalls in the barn were filled with fresh, fluffy pine shavings. Raine had worked without complaint doing *his* work, which left him feeling like an ass. In trying to do the right thing out of respect for his boss—and her—he was unfairly taking out his frustrations on her.

Only now he had her good and annoyed with him, and she didn't bother to hide it as they made their way out to the arena for their morning training session.

He hoped their talk last night helped breakthrough the mental barrier she had over that one vertical jump, and watched carefully for any signs of distress as she and Diamond Fire warmed up.

Everything seemed okay, until he walked her through the new course he'd set up earlier that morning. Accusation and anxiety filled her silence when her glare told him she recognized he'd replicated the course from the day of their wreck back in December.

Ignoring that, he signaled for her to run it through. As they started, he could see horse and rider were equally edgy, only he wasn't so sure if Fire was picking up her anxiety, or remembering the fall himself. When they approached the final turn, the gelding took the bit and blew right past the vertical. Raine brought him back under control at the far side of the arena. She twirled him around in a few tight, fast circles, her displeasure with her mount abundantly clear.

Fire was breathing fast when she urged him into a canter once around the arena, then turned him back onto the course. Reyes fisted his hands at the obvious discourse between the two. They were fighting each other instead of working together as a team. Raine didn't trust herself, and Fire was losing his trust in her. Anything else today would do more damage than good.

"That's enough," he called out before they reached the final turn. He had to figure out a new tactic before their bond was permanently broken. "We're done for now."

She reined up in surprise, her long braid flipping over her shoulder as her head whipped toward him. "What?"

"Take the rest of the day off," he said.

"I don't understand."

He waved his arm toward the guest house. "Go workout, swim, relax, whatever you want to do. But you're done riding for today."

When he headed back to the barn, she cantered Fire past and whirled him around to block Reyes' path. "Why?"

"Because I said so. We do this my way, remember?"

She glared at him for a long moment, her hazel eyes flashing fire.

"How can I forget?" She backed her horse three

quick paces before spinning him toward the barn. "Apparently *everything* is your way."

Yeah, and sometimes his way sucked.

The thing was, when it came to the *everything* she referred to, not sleeping with her wasn't only about respecting his boss and friend. He'd realized half-way through the night that was really nothing more than a lucky excuse he was holding onto for self-preservation.

He'd felt a pull toward her from the first moment he'd set eyes on her years ago, and each time they met, it only grew stronger. Casual hook-ups had never appealed to him, and if he let himself get too close to her, what the hell was he going to do when she went home to Texas?

Because there was no question she would be going home in three weeks.

He went into the office to finish filing the paperwork for Morning Glory, all the while hyper-aware of the sound of Raine's movements out by the stalls. When it had been quiet for at least fifteen minutes, he figured she'd left and gone back to the guest house.

With nothing else to keep himself busy, he broke down and called Jessica Wills over at Retired Racers. A bump of his elbow knocked over his bottled water just as she answered. He hit the speaker phone button and scrambled for some napkins.

"Good morning, Reyes," the older woman greeted as he wiped up his mess. "I wasn't expecting to hear from you guys until Estefan was back."

They hadn't brought in any more horses for training the past few weeks in anticipation of being shorthanded while his dad was gone. It was supposed to afford Reyes his own semi-vacation. Problem was, he had no desire for extra time on his hands today, or the next three weeks. While he did have the unexpected last minute addition of training Raine and Fire to fill some time, *she* was the exact reason he was desperate for the distraction of a much busier schedule.

"Morning Glory just left with the Hamiltons," he told Jessica. "I'm going to need something challenging to work with over here or I'll be bored out of my mind."

"Tell me why a nice guy like you doesn't have a girlfriend to keep him busy?"

"Horses like me better than women do."

"Quit yanking my chain, Rey," she admonished with a laugh. "We both know that's not true. You know, my cousin's daughter is still single. I'm happy to give you her number."

He made a face at the phone but forced a smile into his voice. "I appreciate the thought, Jess, but I'll be sticking with horses for now. Please tell me you can help me out on that front."

"Well, you know I've always got horses for ya'll. There's two here in particular I've been holding for you if you want to pop on over."

"Perfect. I'll bring the trailer."

Reyes hung up and tossed the soggy napkins in the garbage. Then he swiped his keys off the desk on his way out the door to hook up the horse trailer. His pulse jolted at the sight of Raine leaning against the wall outside the office door, and he jerked to a stop with a muttered curse.

"Fire and I aren't challenging enough for you?" she accused.

Realizing she heard everything from the speaker phone, he shot back, "You hang around just to eavesdrop?"

Guilt flickered before she pushed away from the wall. "I wanted to talk to you."

"Well, that's a switch." He angled past her to head outside to his Jeep.

"Are you really that mad about what happened last night?" she asked from right behind him. "Because if that's the problem here this morning, I'll apologize. Again."

"I'm not mad at you."

"You're sure acting like it over one little kiss."

Geezus, that had been so much more than a *little* kiss. He opened his door, then thought better of it and slammed it shut again to face her. "I live in Colorado. You live in Texas."

"And?"

"I don't screw around just to screw around. Never have, never will."

"Neither do I." Her gaze met his for a moment, then faltered. She stuffed her hands in her front pockets and turned to lean her butt against the front tire fender while hunching her shoulders. Her gaze met his, then bounced away to look out over the mountains to the west. "So, I guess I do owe you another apology. I was scared. I *am* scared—about a lot of things. I was using you as a distraction to keep from facing some hard questions, and I'm sorry."

He should be offended by that, shouldn't he? No one liked to be used. He definitely should not be thinking about offering himself up as a willing distraction whenever she needed one. Hopefully often.

For the next three weeks, anyway.

He gave himself a hard mental shake and reached for his door once more. "Don't worry about it. Apology accepted."

As he opened the door, she straightened from the side of his Jeep. "Are you going to get more rescue horses?"

Despite her already knowing that answer, he gave a curt, "Yeah."

"Can I come with you?"

"No."

"Please?"

Halfway onto the driver's seat, he paused with a frown. The less time they spent together the better. "Don't you have a three hour workout to get done?"

She gave him an innocent little smile. "My trainer gave me the rest of the day off."

Idiot.

"Then go shopping or something," he said impatiently. "Meet your friends for lunch."

"That's totally sexist. Besides, I hate shopping, and all my friends are in Texas, remember?"

Damn it all anyway. He scrambled to come up with a good suggestion. Anything to keep from being closed up in a vehicle with her for an extended period of time. As if the overwhelming attraction wasn't bad enough, she wasn't quite the spoiled little rich girl he'd imagined, and he liked the woman he was getting to know. "Go visit your cousins then."

"They're all working. Besides, I want to see where you get the horses from and learn more about the whole process."

And he didn't want to bond with her over the rescue horses.

"Come on, Reyes," she pleaded, looking up at him through her lashes. "If *you're* bored, imagine how I feel, all by myself, all this way from home."

That last bit was laying it on a bit thick. She knew it. He knew it. And yet there he was, feeling the corner of his mouth tug upward before he could force it back into a forbidding line.

Raine's eyes lit up, and she hurried around to the passenger side of his Jeep.

Sonofabitch. "I did not say yes."

Undeterred by his stern voice, she flashed him a saucy grin as she opened the door. "Yes you did. But I promise, I'll keep my hands to myself."

95

"That's not what I'm worried about."

She muttered what sounded like, *"Maybe you should be,"* under her breath, but the slamming of the door drowned out the words, and he wasn't stupid enough to ask her to repeat them. He was already in enough trouble.

*R*aine snuck a glance at Reyes' solemn profile as he made the turn out of the estate's gated driveway. He'd been grumpy all morning. His attitude had annoyed her at first, but while brushing Fire after their disastrous training session, her rational brain had finally managed to remind her he'd broken things off last night because he was a good guy. An honorable guy.

So, she switched her mood and found a little teasing had coaxed a peek at his reluctant humor. Very reluctant, and a very short peek. But still.

"I don't screw around."

She respected the hell out of that. Too many men in her circle at home and on the jumping circuit were only about screwing around. The guys at home were spoiled, rich playboys who used their money and status to get women into bed. Many on the circuit were mostly looking for a good time in the moment, because the time span between events made relationships difficult. On the flip side, others cheated on wives or girlfriends, because sometimes they were away from home for weeks at a time.

Either way, she'd learned early on it wasn't how she wanted to live her life. Last night with Reyes—acting first on the siren call of their sizzling attraction—had been a first for her, and after realizing how her actions had come across, it was a last, too.

She couldn't shake how his voice sounded when he'd told her he needed this job. *Because* of what had happened to him. And she got to thinking that even though she was still insanely attracted to him, maybe they could be friends. A guy with his depth of integrity was someone she'd like to have as a friend. Plus, she had a feeling he could use one who understood he'd gone through some crappy shit, because she sure did.

Maybe he had one already. Heck, maybe he had a whole bunch already from the Army, but a person could never have enough friends, could they?

"Do horses really like you better than women?" she asked to break the silence.

He shot her a sideways glance before giving a slight shake of his head. "I distinctly recall your palm smacking my cheek only seconds after you telling me you didn't like me."

"I didn't know you yet," she said with an unapologetic shrug. "Besides, you dared me."

"Don't dare a Diamond," he mocked lightly. "I should've dared you to stay back at the estate."

"Why? Are you afraid if you spend time with me you'll like me?"

That got her another sharp glance from him, but he didn't answer as he rested his wrist over the top of the steering wheel and watched the road.

"I dare you to answer," she taunted. "*Truthfully*."

"I'm not a Diamond."

"So you don't take dares?"

His lips curved into a smile. "I'm not ten years old anymore."

"My brothers still dare each other, and they're all older than me—*and* you're avoiding the question."

He shrugged.

She was trying to come up with something clever when his low voice reached across the cab.

"I already like you, Raine. That's the problem."

After a quick glance, she watched the passing scenery. "Does it have to be a problem? Because I like you, too, so why can't we at least be friends?"

"I don't usually want to kiss my friends. Do you?"

"No, but there's a first time for everything." She hoped the smile she shot his way did not reveal the nerves churning in her stomach. "We could give it a shot."

"Easier said than done."

"Come on. How hard can it be?"

The moment the question left her mouth, heat

99

flashed through her from head to toe. He'd been *very* hard when she was plastered against his body in the pool. In the split second her gaze met his, she was certain he was remembering the exact same thing. She still wanted to kiss him plus a whole lot more.

She bit her lip and turned her flaming face to the window. "Maybe you should just tell me about where we're going and the horse rescue."

After a moment of silence, he cleared his throat and told her all about Retired Racers, Jessica Wills, and the operation she'd been running for nearly ten years. Raine ignored a little spike of jealousy when she thought of the woman's offer of her cousin's daughter's phone number. He'd turned her down anyway, so there was nothing to be jealous of, right?

Right.

It turned out *"pop on over"* ended up being almost a forty minute drive before Reyes turned onto a pine tree-lined drive bordered by pastures with white fences, and more than two dozen grazing horses dotting the green land.

He parked in front of a huge hunter green stable with five roof dormers on each side, and white trim all around. By the time they got out of the Jeep, a tall, slim blond woman in a yellow T-shirt, jeans, and cowboy boots exited the open doors and approached with a wide smile. Reyes had said Jessica was in her mid-fifties, but Raine wouldn't have guessed her to be a day over forty.

The woman gave him a hug and a kiss on the cheek before the two turned to her, and he made introductions.

Raine shook her hand as the woman eyed her with open curiosity. "Reyes told me all about Retired Racers on the way here. This place is very impressive."

"Thanks." Jessica twisted at the waist, her gaze sweeping toward the barn and back. "This is what my ex-husband gets for being a no-good, cheating sonofabitch."

Raine couldn't stop a high eyebrow arch, and the blond laughed.

"Jess has no filter," Reyes warned with a smile. "You get used to it."

"Too bad Thomas didn't." Jessica turned for the barn. "Oh well. His loss."

"Clearly," Raine murmured with a grin. She liked her—filter be damned.

On their way inside, the woman waved her hand in the general direction of the two of them. "What's going on here?" Her gaze settled on Reyes. "Is this English filly why you won't let me fix you up?"

English filly? Raine nearly choked on a surprised laugh, though she assumed her dark gray breeches and black riding boots had sparked the silly description.

"Raine and I are…friends."

Jessica laughed with clear disbelief. "Right. And I'm the bloody queen of England." Before either of them could reply, the blond stopped in front of a stall where a tall, black thoroughbred had its head extended over the door, curious brown eyes watching the three of them. "Anyway, this lady here is Willow Moonlight, and next to her is Saving Grace."

Raine grinned at the names. She absolutely loved the creativity involved in naming horses—especially thoroughbred race horses. Moving over to the bay mare's stall, she rubbed her forehead while Jessica went over what she knew of each horse's history.

Each had been with her for nearly two months to rest and de-stress after varying success at the track. Willow had been over-trained after her winning streak waned, and Saving Grace had needed a low-impact environment to recover from a gastric ulcer. Both situations were something Raine had heard of in her field as well, though careful monitoring ensured her horses never reached a level where drastic intervention was required.

Jessica explained sometimes a horse needed to just be a horse instead of a high-performance athlete. Eat grass, doze in the sunshine, run through a green pasture. Some could go back, while most 'retired' to a new life, transitioning into lower-stress careers.

Listening to her and Reyes discuss possible paths for each thoroughbred gave Raine a new level of appreciation for his skill and knowledge. It was obvious he earned respect from everyone he worked with. Uncle Mark and Aunt Janine. The Hamiltons. Jessica.

Recognizing the depth of their confidence in him, she realized she'd been holding back during their training sessions. She hadn't trusted that he knew enough to truly be of any help to her and Fire. How could he when he had no experience with riders, and she hadn't actually witnessed proof of his results with horses?

But last night proved his instincts were dead on. In the dead of night, she accepted the fact she needed to face her fear of that one stupid jump. Things hadn't gone so well that morning, but it was time for her to confront what had happened head on, not forget it.

And if she was going to make forward progress, she needed to fully trust Reyes to do what was best for her and her horse. Because he'd also proved last night, and today, he had her best interests at heart—not his own.

11

*R*eyes put the last of the horses out to pasture Saturday morning, and then found a western saddle similar to his to fit Diamond Fire. Taz was all ready to go, and he was tightening Fire's cinch when Raine arrived for her training session a few minutes later.

His pulse gave the usual excited skip as he swept his gaze over her standard uniform of T-shirt, breeches, boots, and braid. Then again, there was nothing standard about her ass in those breeches. They were killing him every single day—though, far be it for him to complain.

She, however, eyed the western saddle with a frown. "Why is he wearing that?"

"We're going for a trail ride."

Her gaze shifted from Fire to Taz and back. "What about training?"

He finished with the cinch and flipped the stirrup down from over the seat. "When's the last time you rode Fire for fun?"

She arched her brow. "He's not a pleasure horse."

"No, but he still needs to be a horse, doesn't he?" He saw understanding dawn in her expression just before she averted her gaze and moved toward the gelding's head to stroke her hand down his nose.

"Fire gets plenty of rest between events." Her voice had a defensive edge. "We take good care of our horses."

"I didn't mean to imply you don't, but after picking up Willow and Grace from Jessica's yesterday, I realized maybe Fire needs to de-stress a little like the thoroughbreds do. Maybe you both do." He leaned in to see her face over the saddle. "Did you take any time off after the accident?"

"Eight weeks after my shoulder surgery," she said.

"Besides that," he clarified. "Did you take any time to just ride him and relax? Maybe rebuild the bond the two of you have?"

Raine frowned, her gaze locked on Fire. "Once I could ride again, there wasn't any time," she said softly. "One of our junior riders kept him in jumping condition, and when the doctor cleared me, we went right back into practice to catch up for the beginning of the season."

Guilt darkened her hazel eyes to almost brown when she finally looked at him. He moved around to the front of her horse and handed her the reins with a smile. "Well, then today we're just riding. I hope you like ham sandwiches, because I packed a lunch."

Surprise touched her features. "How long are we going to be gone?"

"'Til at least mid-afternoon."

"That long? Are there bathrooms along the way?"

He laughed at her pink cheeks and patted the leather bags secured to Taz's saddle. "I've got all the necessities right here."

Toilet paper. Hand wipes. Lunch. Water. Picnic blanket.

Everything except condoms. He would be lying if he said the thought hadn't crossed his mind, but since they were doing the friendship thing in addition to training, he needed to provide obstacles to temptation wherever possible.

They led the horses from the barn, and he glanced over as the breeze blew a loose strand of hair across Raine's face. He tightened his hands on the reins, suppressing the urge to reach out and tuck it behind her ear. If he did that, he'd want to cup the back of her head so he could lean down and cover her mouth with his to see if there was any flavor to that gloss making her lips so shiny.

And on that note, he'd now be finding a log or a boulder to sit on while they ate their lunch and leave the picnic blanket packed deep in his saddle bag.

He'd chosen a longer trail that looped east onto

public land bordering the Diamond estate before connecting with the trails on the west side of the property. As they rode past the huge main house, he noticed Raine's gaze sweeping over the estate. He knew her family had plenty of money like his employers, and wondered if their place in Texas was as grand.

"Does it make you miss home?" he asked.

She lifted a shoulder, her head still averted. "I travel enough I'm used to being away."

"That doesn't answer the question."

Now her gaze swung around to him. "I guess not really. It's a lot cooler up here, and I like that for training outside instead of always being in air conditioning or it being super hot outside. Plus, my family has spread out, much like everyone here has. My brothers all moved out years ago, and my parents both travel for work a lot, so it's hit and miss when we see each other. If I miss anything, it's all of them, not the house."

"You still live at home?"

A wry smile curved her lips. "It's where I train, so it's just easier."

"Hey, I live where I work, so I get it."

Her head swung back toward her uncle's one last time before they entered the woods. "I will say, though, I'm not used to it being so quiet around *here*. There was always a full house whenever I visited."

And these days, he was the one with the most

permanent residence at the Diamond estate. "I'm not about to complain about the quiet," he said.

She tossed him a smile. "I suppose not. Though, with Shelby and Dev engaged, I bet it won't be long before you have a niece or nephew running around getting into trouble."

"They're talking about kids already?" The news shouldn't surprise him, but he hadn't thought about being an uncle anytime soon.

"Shelby said they want to be married for a little while first, but I'm sure with Merit and Asher already started, the rest will have kids sooner than later. I know Celia and Robert are trying, and probably Loyal and Roxanna, too."

The wistful note in her voice started his heart beating a little faster. "How about you?"

"Am I trying?" Her dark eyebrows arched over eyes sparkling with humor. "Um, probably best if I get myself a man first, don't you think?"

"Probably." He grinned even as his pulse skipped at the idea of offering himself for the position. "However, I meant in the future. Do you want kids someday?"

"Definitely." She tilted her head sideways, glancing at him from beneath her lashes. "You?"

"Yeah, I hope so." The smile she gave him did funny things to his stomach, and he quickly shifted the conversation. "How many brothers do you have?"

"There's five of us. Axel, the twins—Phoenix and

Chance—and then Olix. I'm the only girl, and the youngest."

"Ahh. That explains so much," he teased.

"Shut up."

He laughed. "I'm the baby, too. I bet you got away with a lot of shit just like me."

"True—but it can suck, too. Especially for girls. I've got four brothers who are super overprotective, and my dad still thinks I'm his baby girl."

"You'll always be his baby girl."

Her nose scrunched up, and he laughed again. Riding like this always brought him peace, but today felt different. Lighter. Fun.

Man, when was the last time he'd truly had fun?

"What about you?" Raine asked. "I know Devante, and don't you have an older sister, too? I think I remember Shelby pointing her out at Loyal's wedding back in February."

"Yeah, Solana. She's an FBI agent based in Washington state, though she's hoping for a transfer to the Colorado field office. We each left the moment we graduated high school, so if she comes back, it'll be nice to all be close again."

"That's cool. That she works for the FBI, I mean."

"It's her job," he said with a shrug.

Raine looked ahead, her expression suddenly pensive. "But it's a job that can make a difference. All I do is ride horses."

He blinked at the statement. "What's wrong with that? I pretty much do the same."

"You train them—there's a difference," she countered. "And you help re-home retired thoroughbreds. Shelby runs her clinic so low income families can have pets and not worry about the cost of caring for them. Loyal and Grayson run the veterans foundation, and Grayson also raises and trains service dogs. What good does me riding a horse over jumps do?"

There was an unexpected depth to her question that had him posing his own. "Would you rather be doing something else?"

"Maybe." As if realizing what she'd just admitted, she shot him a quick glance and a shrug. "I mean, I love what I do, but I guess I wonder sometimes."

"What else would you do?"

She grimaced as her shoulders shook with a visible shiver. "I have no idea."

"Maybe it's something you should think about."

She didn't reply, and they rode in silence until he noticed her rub a palm over her bare arm. He'd thrown a gray plaid button up over his T-shirt this morning, leaving it open and rolling up the sleeves. It kept him comfortable in the shade of the tall trees, but Raine's T-shirt didn't appear to be doing the job.

"You cold?" he asked.

She looked over in surprise and then dropped her hand back down to her leg. "I'll be fine once we're back in the sun. I'm usually warm when I'm jumping, but it's cooler here in the woods than I would've expected."

He should've thought of that and suggested she grab a sweatshirt. Shrugging out of his shirt, he rode closer to hand it over. "Here, put this on."

"What about you?"

"I was actually getting a little warm," he fibbed.

She hesitated one more moment before taking it to slide her arms into the sleeves. "Thanks."

It was huge on her, with the rolled sleeves nearly reaching her wrists. The unbuttoned sides fell down along her thighs in a way that had him imagining her in nothing but his shirt, her dark hair loose and wavy as it cascaded over her shoulders.

He let loose a groan under his breath. She shot him a questioning glance, and heat crept up his neck as he quickly urged Taz ahead of Diamond Fire. If he kept thinking along the lines of her in his shirt, in his bed— *don't go adding details*—the ride was going to very quickly get extremely uncomfortable.

He scrambled for a distraction and went back to what they'd been talking about. "You know, who's to say you can't jump *and* do something more? As you pointed out, the re-homing isn't my whole job."

She and Fire drew even with him and Taz once more. "Can I help you with Saving Grace and Willow Midnight the next couple of weeks?" she asked.

More time together above and beyond her training? Absolutely not. "Sure."

"That would be great." Her hazel eyes lit with a sudden excitement. "If you show me what to do, I could start a program when I get home."

Home. In Texas.

The reminder hit like a kick to the gut.

But then again, considering how much he enjoyed spending time with her yesterday and today, that reminder was exactly what he needed. And often.

12

*R*aine felt a little bad taking her scheduled day off on Sunday when it felt like she'd already taken Friday and Saturday off. But, seeing as those were both on her trainer's orders, she ignored the guilt and headed up to the main house for brunch.

The past few days put a spring in her step. Things had been good. Great even. First at the horse rescue on Friday, and then yesterday's ride had been amazing in a way she hadn't realized how much she and Fire needed. She was pretty sure her horse enjoyed the change of scenery as much as she did, and the company hadn't been too shabby, either.

She rolled her eyes at her understatement and lifted a hand to keep her loose hair from blowing into her face. Reyes had been nice, and fun, and surprisingly funny at times. They'd talked comfortably the whole time, and she didn't think he'd caught any of the countless instances she'd discretely lifted the collar of his shirt to inhale the tummy-flipping scent of him clinging to the material.

At least she sure hoped not, since she was the one who suggested they be friends. The very last thing she should've been doing as they ate lunch on a big fallen log was imagine sliding over to bury her nose in the crook of his neck—but dear Lord, the man smelled so damn *good.*

Doing her best to put him out of her mind, she walked past all the vehicles in the drive and entered the house. A cacophony of voices led her to the kitchen. Of the dozen or so people gathered, her gaze landed smack dab on Reyes holding Ava, Asher and Honor's little four month old.

Her heart lodged up in her throat at the sight of his uninhibited smile as the baby giggled while he ran her tiny little palm over the whiskers on his chin.

"Hey."

Raine jumped at the stage whisper in her ear, and twisted to see her cousin standing slightly behind her with a wide grin.

"I'm telling you," Shelby said in a soft sing-song voice, "there's something about those Torrez boys."

Yes, there definitely was. Looking back toward Reyes and the baby, she gave Bells a one-armed hug. "Only they're not boys anymore."

"Most definitely not," her cousin agreed with a happy grin.

A spark of envy burned in her chest. Not for her cousin's man, but because if she was being honest and said to hell with all the friendship stuff, she wanted what Shelby had.

With Reyes.

And yet, it wasn't going to happen. They lived in different states. Hell, they lived different lives.

Not that different.

Different enough though.

"You know, we've invited Reyes to brunch before. This is the first time he's come."

Her pulse skipped at her cousin's insinuation. She glanced at Shelby, then back to him. "We're becoming friends."

"Just friends?"

"There's no point in anything more." She didn't bother to hide the disappointment in her voice, and Shelby squeezed her shoulder in commiseration. "Neither of us is into casual flings, and other than this one month, our lives are hundreds of miles apart."

"Hmm. That's a shame. The miles apart that is—not the casual stuff."

You're telling me.

Someone called her name, and as she turned to look, Reyes' lashes lifted and their gazes connected. Her heart thumped hard. Seconds ticked by as the world shifted beneath her feet while undeniable yearning made it hard to swallow.

"A real shame," Shelby whispered before walking between them.

She blinked as the connection was broken, and then her cousin Merit stepped up to envelop her in a bear hug. Raine spent the next five minutes making her way around the island and table, giving hugs to everyone. Grandma and Grandpa, Asher and Honor, Devante, Celia and Robert, Merit, Mae, and Ian, and last but not least, Loyal and Roxanna.

Merit and Mae's little guy Maverick was firmly ensconced in Grandma Irene's arms, so she turned to Reyes, who still held Ava. "My turn."

He twisted away with a teasing smile. "I just got her."

"I haven't even met her."

"Fine, you win."

She leaned forward to take the baby, her pulse kicking up when his large hands brushed against hers in the exchange. She focused on Ava, teasing and tickling to make her smile and giggle. Asher and Honor watched from over by the island, but the two seemed content with having a break.

After a few minutes, the baby fussed and twisted in her arms, so she turned her around to face all the action. When Reyes held out a rattle, Ava seized it and shook her little fist with gusto. After the first smack to her face, Raine laughed before ducking backward to avoid a second. Reyes was quick to switch the rattle for a stuffed animal.

"Good call," she said with a smile of thanks. "I didn't know you were going to be here."

"Dev made me come."

His wry tone had her arching her brows.

He rolled his eyes the tiniest bit. "He thinks I need to socialize more."

Despite their acrimonious start earlier in the week—and last summer—anytime she'd seen him interact with other people, he seemed friendly and outgoing. But after their talk at the pool, she was pretty sure she could read between the lines. "Because of...?"

His eyes were a dark shade of green, solemn and shadowed. "Yeah." He shifted his gaze to the baby and reached out to let Ava wrap her tiny hand around his finger. "He's not wrong."

Sympathy pulsed with each heavy thump of her heart. Yet another reason they couldn't act on the chemistry between them—she wouldn't be the one to screw up a job that helped him deal with the horror he'd lived through.

So...friends it would be.

She leaned the baby in to plant a slobbery kiss on his cheek as she said, "Then I'm glad you're here."

13

*E*motion swelled in Reyes' chest at Raine's soft statement. Other than his brother, she was the only one here who knew exactly what he'd gone through. Well, he suspected Dev had told Shelby some, but he'd never talked to her about it himself.

Yesterday, he'd spent the entire day without any heavy moments cutting off his air until later in the evening when he laid in bed and tried to turn the light off for the first time in months. It took all of five seconds before he had to flip it back on, but at least as he drifted off to a replay of the day spent with Raine, he'd gotten a restful night's sleep.

While he had told her his brother made him come today, knowing she was going to be there, he hadn't scrambled for an excuse when the invite was issued. And Dev was also right that he needed to stop isolating himself at the stables with the horses. Other than the

Diamonds, he hadn't taken any time to reconnect with high school friends still in the area, and he only texted his Army buddies every so often.

Sitting at brunch with all of the new, happy families, watching how cute Maverick and Ava were as they interacted with everyone, he found himself yearning for more in his own life. And with that yearning, he couldn't help watching and listening to Raine across the table during brunch, and later, when everyone pitched in to clean up after the meal.

She was a vision with her loose hair falling in soft waves past her shoulders. A gauzy, mint shirt brought out the green in her hazel eyes, and a pair of white jean capris showed off her great ass and legs. Hell, even the gold sandals on her small feet were enough to make his pulse skip.

Stop looking.

Right. Like that was gonna happen.

He grabbed a towel to dry dishes as Asher washed and Merit rinsed, his gaze straying to Raine as often as possible without being too obvious. Even though it wasn't quite a week ago, it was hard to recall back when he thought she was a spoiled little rich girl. Yeah, she'd had her moments, but he'd also seen her work hard both in the ring and cleaning stalls, and with her own personal workouts. She was determined and dedicated, and he had no doubt she was going to ride Fire all the way to gold someday.

Which meant it would be stupid to imagine her in

any way as part of his new-found desire for more in his life.

Dev carried the last of the dirty plates to set on the counter for Asher to wash, then grabbed a towel to help dry. "It would appear you and Raine called a truce," he observed in a low voice.

"For the most part."

"A truce?" Merit glanced over. "What were you two fighting about?"

Reyes grimaced. Talking about Raine in front of Merit and Asher—and damn it, here came Loyal—was not something he wanted to do. "Not fighting. More like not seeing eye to eye on her training. It's fine though. We're good."

"Well, I don't envy you. Raine can be stubborn as all hell." Merit handed him another dish as Loyal leaned his butt against the island. "When we were visiting them in Texas one summer, we were all playing hide and seek and ended up looking for her until after midnight."

"I remember that," Loyal groused.

"Did she get lost?" Reyes asked.

"No." Asher chuckled. "She just refused to come out until we found her."

"Even after we called out the game was over."

"I think she was six at the time," Loyal said. "*We* were all worried she was lost and afraid in the dark, but when she found out she was the last to be found, she declared victory."

"Uncle Matt always said she takes after her name."

Asher and Merit exchanged a smile and they both said together, *"Can't stop rain."*

Reyes shifted his gaze to Raine just as her head whipped around.

"Oh my God—what are you guys talking about?" she hollered from the other side of the kitchen.

"Want to play hide and seek?" Merit teased.

She rolled her eyes, though a smile tugged at her lips. "Say what you want, I beat all of you guys *and* my brothers that night."

Loyal pushed away from the island and went to lift Maverick out of Robert's arms. "First and last time we ever played hide and seek with Raine. But we'll play with you some day, little man."

The baby grinned, drool wetting his chin as well as the hand stuffed in his mouth. He was six months old, but having been born seven weeks early, he and Ava were near the same size despite the two months difference between their birthdays.

"It's not my fault you guys were sore losers," Raine retorted.

Celia and Shelby jumped into the fray as the cousins continued to tease each other while Grandma Irene tossed in a story or two about Raine's dad and the senator. Reyes kept drying, smiling as he listened to them joke about her side of the family's ridiculous obsession with dares. It made him think of when she smacked him across the face last week.

"You know what you're doing?"

Reyes winced at his brother's low voice beside him. He didn't need to ask what Dev meant; he heard the real question in his tone.

"We're friends," he said, as much for his brother as himself.

"You don't look at her like a friend."

Yeah, Dev saw him watching her. Wanting her.

What he didn't know was how damn hard he was fighting to not fall for her.

14

*R*eyes mentally psyched himself up for the Monday morning session with Raine while turning the horses out and cleaning stalls. Being friends with her, getting to know her and *really* liking who she was wasn't working for him.

Or, more accurately, it was working too well.

Yesterday, he'd left shortly after brunch and stayed away from the estate until evening chores. Today, his goal was to get her over the damn jump. The sooner she was over it and back to her regular training schedule, the sooner she could go home, and the less danger he would be in.

The light tick of boot heels on cement gave him a three second warning before Raine called out, "Good morning!"

Damn it, she was early. Though, to be fair, she'd been early every single morning.

Reyes glanced up as she came to a stop at the stall door, one hand hooked around the beam that rose to the rafters as she leaned into the opening, her braid dangling over her shoulder. He tried, but couldn't stop his gaze from taking in the snug fit of her white T-shirt, black breeches, and shiny black boots.

"Where'd you go yesterday?" she asked as he threw another scoop of dirty bedding into the wheel barrow.

"Out."

It came out harsher than he intended, and surprise flickered in her expression before she lifted her chin slightly. "Well, Fire and I went for another ride yesterday. Just the two of us, and it was nice."

"Good. Then you should be all ready to work today."

"I've been ready to work every day." Resentment edged her voice.

"And yet there you stand."

He expected her to whirl around and storm off. Instead, she straightened and pinned him with her gaze. "So, that's how you're going to play it? Like this weekend never happened?"

"Nothing did happen."

Except it had. They'd spent most of Friday and Saturday together, and Sunday brunch, all without a single note of animosity. Friendship had definitely been in the works.

"All right then," she said. "My mistake."

He had to turn away from the hurt in her eyes and was relieved when he heard her footsteps retreat. He finished cleaning the stall before meeting her out in the arena at eight a.m., where she and Fire were already warming up.

Keeping his tone businesslike, he called out instructions and suggestions on a few of their sloppier efforts. When she avoided the vertical jump on the first round, he let it pass. After the second pass, he huffed out a sigh under his breath.

"You can't keep avoiding the jump, Raine."

"I'm working up to it," she shot back with an icy glare.

"I thought you were a professional, but I could dare you if that helps."

"I don't need you to dare me."

The elevated tone of her voice revealed her anxiety. Reyes raked a hand through his hair as he raised his hand for her to stop. When she reined her horse to a halt in front of him, he moved closer to stroke the gelding's neck while looking up at her.

"You know this is all in your head, right?" Anger flashed in her expression, and he reached his other hand to rest on her knee. "I'm not saying what you're feeling isn't valid, but physically, there's nothing keeping you from doing this."

"You think I don't know that? I hate this as much as everyone else." As soon as the words were out, she averted her gaze. Her fingers held the reins in a death grip, and her gelding sidled sideways a step before she halted him.

Reyes moved close again. "Do you trust Fire?"

"Of course I do."

He shook his head at her automatic reply. "I'm not looking for the answer you think I want to hear. Think about it first, then tell me if you truly trust your horse."

Her gaze held his for a long moment before she leaned forward, almost hugging the gelding's neck as she rubbed her palm over his shiny coat. "Yes, I trust him."

"Then let *him* take you over the jump. Don't worry about counting strides or anything else. Close your eyes if you have to. Just give him the reins and let him take you over."

Raine slowly sat up straight in the saddle. The breath she released was uneven, her gaze apprehensive, but she nodded. He gave her knee an encouraging squeeze a second before she pivoted Fire away. She cantered him around the arena once and then lined up with the jump.

"Don't think about it," Reyes whispered. *"Just ride."*

His pulse pounded hard with each stride Fire took toward the jump. Raine's posture was tense, but her rhythm with the horse was matched perfectly. The closer they got, the farther he leaned in, willing them to sail right over.

It's time.

Come on, Raine. You got this.

One stride before the vertical, she bent forward over Fire's neck—and Reyes' gut clenched when he saw how far. *Too far.* Her gelding took the jump, but his front feet nicked the top rail, bouncing it from the cups holding it in place. As he came down on the other side with a hard stumble, Raine pitched forward way too far to keep her seat.

Sonofabitch!

Reyes took off at a dead run, heart jammed up into his throat when he saw her leave the saddle. He shouldn't have pushed her. If she got hurt because of him—

Fire came to a choppy halt with Raine bear-hugging his neck, her body dangling in front of him. Reyes reached them as she let go to put her feet on the ground. He gripped her shoulders to turn her toward him, his frantic gaze searching for any injuries.

"You okay? Are you hurt?"

Despite her head shake, her eyes shimmered with tears. Her whole body shook as he pulled her into his arms. He hugged her tight in an attempt to ward off a huge wave of guilt. If her legs had gotten tangled up in Fire's—

"I'm okay." Raine's voice was muffled against his chest with her helmet tucked under his chin.

"I shouldn't have pushed so hard."

"It's okay." When he instinctively tightened his

hold, she added, "Really. And we finally made it over, at least."

"Yeah, you did." Major relief allowed a small smile. "I'm proud of you. Though, I would not recommend doing it *that way* in competition."

She gave his chest a little shove and snuck a hand up to wipe at her cheek. "Don't make fun of me."

"Never." He leaned back to assure her that's not what he intended. Seeing the tremulous smile on her lips, his breath caught. When her lashes rose and her still-teary gaze met his, all rational thought fled.

He lifted both hands to her face as he crushed his mouth down on hers.

All the emotions jumbled up inside him—relief she hadn't been hurt, days of wanting this, and more—and it all took him from zero to sixty in seconds flat.

He angled his head to deepen the kiss, and Raine was right there with him. Her tongue met his stroke for stroke while her fingers fisted in his shirt, hanging on and pulling him closer at the same time.

A hint of mint teased his senses and had him searching for more. He swept his hands down her back, molding her curves to his chest, cupping her ass in those second-skin breeches. Her breathy little whimper penetrated the foggy haze of desire. The needy sound made his pulse surge in excitement while at the same time it gave him a cold dousing of reality.

Nothing had changed between them. If anything,

now that she'd conquered the jump, she'd likely be leaving sooner.

Reyes forced himself to drag his mouth from hers. "I'm sorry," he breathed roughly. "I shouldn't have done that."

She went completely still. The hands fisted in his shirt tightened for a moment, then flattened and pushed against his chest. Reminded he still held her tight against him, Reyes let go and stepped back so she was out of reach.

"No…we shouldn't have," she agreed.

Her use of *we* took equal blame, and when her darkened gaze rose to his, it took everything he had not to claim her glistening, swollen lips with his once more. "I'm sorry."

"You said that already." Jaw tight, she reached for the reins. "Forget it."

Fat chance of that.

"I'm going to do flatwork for a bit and then maybe try the jump one more time."

He nodded, but she'd already turned back to her horse. He gave her a leg up into the saddle, then moved to the center of the arena to do the job Mark was paying him to do. Fortunately, Raine was focused on her job, because his thoughts were racing like mad.

Being friends wasn't working.

What had just happened wasn't going to work either.

So what the fuck did he do now?

15

It was nearing eleven p.m. Friday when Raine returned from an extremely extended happy hour with her cousins and cousins-in-law. Though the barn was visible in her peripheral vision, it took everything she had not to glance over as she drove toward the guest house in her aunt's Mercedes. She had to be done letting thoughts of Reyes take over every waking moment of her life.

Then she went and disobeyed and scowled out the driver's side window anyway.

Yep, all the lights above the barn were blazing.

Was he up, or sleeping like a baby? Probably the latter. Because he didn't have anything to keep him up, did he?

Other than the dark.

She forced her gaze away and parked inside the guest house garage while trying to ignore a twinge of sympathy. He clearly didn't want any compassion from her. Didn't seem he wanted anything from her.

It had been four days since Reyes had kissed her in the arena—and she knew damn well that should not be the marker for counting the passage of time. It should be twelve days since she had arrived in Colorado. Or sixteen days until she went home to Texas. Not four flippin' days since Reyes kissed her when ever since then, *he* acted like it hadn't even happened.

Sympathy vanished and a slam of the car door wasn't the least bit satisfactory.

Every time she walked into the barn, the second she laid eyes on the man, the little anticipatory butterflies in her stomach turned into a whirlwind. She practically drooled when he tossed hay bales around like they weighed five pounds instead of fifty. And yesterday, when he leaned close in the office while going over all the paperwork involved in the horse rescue, she'd had to lean against the desk for support because his outdoorsy, manly scent stole her breath and left her light-headed.

Or it might have been the sight of his exposed forearms lined with veins and thick, sinewy muscles that weakened her knees.

Whatever, it was all downright annoying when he treated her as nothing more than a business acquaintance. Whether he was explaining the adoption procedures Aunt Janine had put in place years ago, or calling out instructions as they worked together with one of the new thoroughbreds, his voice—and the rest of him— remained agonizingly unaffected.

As if he hadn't seen her half naked in the pool as his erection throbbed against her core. As if he hadn't kissed her senseless in the arena and hauled her so tight against him she'd felt the thud of his racing heart against her breast.

How the hell did he just turn it off like that?

These days, the only time warmth bled into his voice was when she and Fire had a particularly good run in the arena. Like a dog salivating over a bone, the promise of that glimmer of emotion from him had her working extra hard every day to push herself and her horse to the next level. Hearing the pride in Reyes' voice when he praised their progress was like being bathed in a brilliant ray of sunshine.

She scrunched up her nose as she tossed her purse on the kitchen island and plugged the charger into her nearly dead phone. "You sound like an idiot, thinking like that."

Touring Shelby's Must Love Paws veterinary clinic before relaxing with all the girls on the rooftop bar facing the Rocky Mountains was supposed to have helped her gain some control over her stupid obsession with the man. Instead, she'd listened to Shelby, Celia, Mae, Roxanna, and Honor and found herself reevaluating her life. Well, actually, she'd been thinking about her future since that ride with Reyes her first weekend.

Show jumping didn't age people out early like

many other sports. In fact, many of the top riders were well into their forties, and even their fifties. She could very well have a long and fruitful jumping career if she wanted. She just wasn't so sure that's what she wanted anymore. Even *after* conquering the jump again.

The idea of starting her own rescue gave her a renewed sense of excitement about the future. Something to give her purpose and feel good about at the end of the day.

She started toward the bedroom when her phone buzzed and drew her back to the island counter. The sight of her father's face on the screen skipped her pulse as she answered the call and put him on speaker. "Hi, Dad. Is everything okay?"

"Of course. Why would you ask that?"

"Because it's after eleven?" And for as long as she could remember, he went to bed at nine-forty-five every night like clockwork.

"I just wanted to see how everything is going up there. Are you making progress?"

He voiced it as a question, but the firm expectation in his voice came across almost as a warning. *You better be making progress or else.*

She wanted to ask, *"Or else what, Dad?"* Instead, she consciously unclenched her jaw and sucked in a calming breath before answering. "We are. In fact, we're clearing all the jumps without any more issues."

Thanks to Reyes. A pulse of warmth spread in her

133

chest even though she was still thoroughly annoyed with the distance he kept between them.

"Good," her dad replied. "Exactly what I wanted to hear. I'll call the transport company to schedule your return trip for Monday."

Her pulse lurched as her stomach dropped. "This Monday? Like in three days?"

"Yes."

"But I still have two weeks left." A protest she never thought she'd voice two weeks ago.

"What do you need them for?" her dad asked, a frown evident in his stern tone. "If the problem is fixed, you can come home and get back to work."

Raine stiffened, her jaw clenched once more. "I haven't stopped working, Daddy, and Fire and I are doing better than ever." The force of his silence had her pulse speeding up and she scrambled for something to convince him. She wasn't ready to go home yet. "You were right that the change of scenery would be good for us. Reyes is really good with Fire, and I want to see how far we can get with the time that's left."

"I don't like you being out of competition this long."

She rolled her eyes toward the ceiling in frustration. "That's what I said when you ordered me up here for a full month. But I still came. Now things are going good and I need *you* to trust that I'm doing what is best for me and Fire and our future. Please."

After another moment of hesitation, a grudging grunt of concession came across the line. "Okay, then.

I'll schedule the transport for two weeks from now and send you the details."

Relief had her leaning forward onto her forearms on the counter. "Thank you. And don't worry, I promise you'll be impressed when you see us next."

"I better be."

"You will." She fiddled with the charger cord. "If there's nothing else, I have to be down at the barn by eight, so I should get to bed. Say hi to Mom, and love you both."

"Love you, too, sweetheart. I'll talk to you soon."

Raine disconnected the call and pushed up with her palms flat on the counter as she blew out a breath. She had not expected the panic that had hit at the thought of going home early. She hadn't lied when she told her dad she wanted more training time, but she hadn't been completely truthful, either. It wasn't only the training, it was Reyes. Despite the impenetrable wall he'd erected between them, she still looked forward to seeing him each day, and not only because he was so damn sexy.

After their initial butting of heads, they'd had a couple of good days that first week, and when she wasn't so frickin' hyper aware of him as a man, she thoroughly enjoyed learning about the horses and the rescue operation from him.

She made her way over to the patio doors that offered a clear view of the barn with the upstairs apartment still lit up in the dark of night. There was a lot more to learn before she left—about the horse rescue, and about Reyes. And maybe that was her problem. After that second kiss, she'd been focusing too much on the sizzling physical undercurrents when she should be concentrating on the friendship aspect. She had two weeks to scale his wall, and like with the jump, instinct told her failure wasn't an option.

16

Three weeks into her stay, and Reyes still couldn't force his gaze away from the sway of Raine's ass as she left the barn on her way back to the guest house after practice. One more week. He just had to hang on for one more week and life would go back to normal.

He snorted at his wishful thinking before taking a couple of brushes to Taz's stall. The woman had slowly been driving him insane over the past week and he desperately needed some stress relief. Last time he tried cleaning tack, she'd grabbed a clean cloth and joined him. Watching her rub the leather turned him on while she peppered him with endless questions on the horse rescue operation.

She took in everything he shared with her and kept asking for more. His heart greedily hoarded every second they spent together, because it was killing him to keep her at arm's length and act as if her going home to Texas in one more week was no big deal.

Taz gave a soft wicker as he entered the stall, and Reyes offered the thoroughbred a couple sugar cubes and a firm forehead rub. Then he settled in with a brush in each hand; curry comb in one, dandy brush in the other. Unfortunately, the rhythmic motions over the gelding's silken hide didn't offer the usual meditation effects as his mind remained firmly fixed on Raine.

Not only did she tempt him every damn second of every damn day in those curve-hugging T-shirts and skin tight breeches, but as he'd feared the first week, he found he really, *really* liked her. He respected her work ethic and was impressed with her thorough approach to learning about the rescue, as well as her intuitive suggestions from a different perspective. He'd be talking to Janine about implementing a few of Raine's ideas.

As for the horses, similar to her riding, she possessed a natural talent working with them whether in the saddle or on the ground. Saving Grace and Willow Moonlight were progressing beautifully under her gentle hand.

The woman also had a dry wit that had him fighting hard to keep the barriers up between them. He'd bitten back more grins and laughter in the past week than he had in the past three years. Genuine laughter, not the fake response he'd perfected so everyone would believe everything was okay.

The close quarters of the office were the most difficult. Seduced by her unique floral and horse scent, he used the excuse of paperwork to get close enough to feel her heat, but then had to resist reaching out to skim his rough fingers over her smooth skin. It was pure torture not to touch.

Self-inflicted, sadistic torture.

Yeah, he couldn't wait for her to leave and go back to Texas, and at the same time, he feared once she did, he'd never know normal again.

"So what's RazMaTaz's story?"

Reyes flinched hard at the unexpected sound of Raine's voice at the stall door. With his heart thumping in his chest, he shot her a quick glance. "I thought you left for the day."

Talk about being distracted—he hadn't even heard her boots on the cement.

She slid the stall open to step inside and rub her hand on Taz's forehead. "I forgot my phone in the office."

From the corner of his eye, he watched as she pressed her face into the soft, velvety spot on the side of the thoroughbred's nose and breathed deep while her lashes drifted closed. Her husky hum of contentment slowed his hands as his dick twitched as he imagined her making that sound with her face buried against his neck.

Fuck. He was going to be rock hard in no time if she kept that up.

He moved to Taz's other side and resumed brushing with renewed energy.

Raine ducked under the gelding's neck and came up on the side Reyes had just moved to. "Is he a rescue, too?"

Reyes shifted toward the gelding's hindquarters to keep some distance between them. "Yep. After my discharge from the military, I drove home from Fort Bragg through Lexington and Louisville. I spent a little time at Churchill Downs, just to see where some of Janine's horses came from."

She nodded as she held out her hand in obvious request for one of his brushes. "I'd want to see, too."

So much for stress relief. He passed her the dandy brush, torn between resignation and joy at her company. "The majority of the people treat their horses like royalty," he clarified. "They're their bread and butter—as you well know."

"Of course. But there are always the select assholes who view them as nothing more than a piece of equipment to be used until they stop being profitable."

Yeah, she definitely knew. "That was Taz's owner to a tee. The woman had so much money she could've easily invested the time and money into her horses, but all she cared about was racking up the wins for her stable to elevate her standing in the profession."

"That's pathetic," Raine fumed. "People like that don't even realize that true horsemen see them for the manure they are no matter how many wins they get at the expense of their animals."

Her passion reminded him how wrong he'd been about her at the beginning. "I walked up on an argument between the owner and her trainer about putting Taz down after he'd lost three races in a row."

Her eyes went wide in disbelief. "Like *put him down* put him down?"

"I was just as shocked," Reyes said. "And so furious, I bought him on the spot."

"I would've too." Giving a low growl, she hugged his horse's neck while turning her head to meet his gaze. "Thank God you were there."

The emotion in her eyes had him averting his gaze or risk giving in to the urge to push her up against the wall so he could claim all that passion for himself. "I'd like to think the trainer would've held his ground, but I wasn't taking any chances."

"Did she give you a good deal?"

He snorted. "You'd think, but no. I had to clean out my savings and borrow a couple of grand from Dev." Thirty-five thousand all total. And worth every penny when he considered the hours of therapy Taz had given him. They'd saved each other, really. "Thankfully, the trainer told her where she could shove it and then offered to drive him to Colorado for me, so that helped."

"Surely Aunt Janine would have helped?" she asked as she resumed brushing.

Reyes shrugged. "Probably, but the only thing I

asked for was a place to keep him when we got back."

"And a job?"

"I always had the job."

"Ah." She smoothed the brush over Taz's ribs, the move bringing her closer to where Reyes stood. "Is the woman still in the business?"

A satisfied smile tugged at his mouth as he met her gaze. "Nope. Janine made sure she got out and stayed out. Diamond connections and all."

Raine's answering grin skipped his pulse.

"What about the trainer?" she asked.

"Matt Wesley. He went to work for Big Sur Stables in California. In fact, one of his colts won the Derby last year."

"Good for him. Do you guys keep in touch?"

He nodded. "He sends us horses that need to be rehabbed from time to time."

A soft smile curved her lips as she murmured, "He makes a difference."

Reyes forced his gaze away from her mouth. Since their trail ride when he'd argued she could show jump *and* do something else, she'd gone all in on the rescue route. "I can put you in touch with him, if you want. For when you start your own thing."

"That'd be great." Her gaze lifted, hazel eyes bright with a glimmer of excitement that dimmed slightly as she added, "My dad's probably going to freak out when I tell him what I want to do, but it's not like he can stop me."

Her words said one thing, but there was a hint of a question in her voice, as if she were asking him to back her up.

"You've seen the financials," he reminded, unable to offer false reassurance. "Adoption fees barely cover the cost of the horses and feed. You're going to need your dad's barn—and his staff for when you're away at events."

She was quiet for a long moment. "Not if I buy my own place and hire my own staff."

He arched his brows in surprise. "You could afford that?"

"I have a trust fund," she said nonchalantly.

Right. Of course she did. All the Diamonds probably did.

Raine stood up a little straighter, her shoulders squaring. "I'll put together a detailed business plan and he'll see I've thought it through—that I'm not just jumping in blind. Dad loves a good business plan."

"You ever created a business plan before?"

"Ah...no. Have you?"

He shook his head.

She grimaced, her shoulders drooping before she perked up again. "We've got a whole week to figure it out if you're willing to help me?"

The hope in her voice sent the word *sure* to the tip of his tongue so fast he barely caught it from slipping out. Crafting a business plan would throw them together in close quarters for whole hell of a lot more hours and resisting her was getting harder by the second. But she'd be gone in a week, and the tightness in his chest told him he needed to maintain distance if he wanted his heart intact when she left.

Giving Taz's hind quarters a final swipe, he headed for the stall door as he stated, "Loyal's the one to ask."

Her older cousin was a financial wizard in charge of his own accounting firm and the Cole-Diamond Veterans Foundation, *and* he'd advised both Shelby and Dev while they were setting up their businesses this past spring.

"Yeah, I guess," Raine agreed.

His chest tightened at the disappointment in her voice, but he avoided her gaze as he waited for her to exit the stall before sliding the door closed.

"I'll ask him tonight at Asher and Honor's. Hopefully he'll have some time before I leave."

Reyes clenched his jaw against a wave of guilt and took the brush she thrust in his direction. Her boots sounded behind him on the way to the tack room.

"You know, we're all getting together for dinner tonight. You should come with me."

He admired her tenacity while simultaneously cursing it. The overwhelming desire to take every second with her when he knew it would only hurt him in the end was frustrating.

"I already have plans." To do absolutely fucking nothing, but she didn't have to know that.

"Oh, okay, then." Her voice sounded tight after his curt retort. "Have fun."

He kept his back to her as he straightened the brushes in their bins. "Yep. You, too."

The moment she was gone, he cursed under his breath and swiped up a cloth to start cleaning saddles. They didn't need it, but most of the time on deployment, his guns hadn't either.

He was still at it an hour later when his cell phone vibrated on the office desk. Reyes grimaced when he saw his brother's name.

"What exactly are these plans of yours?" Dev demanded when he answered.

"Hello to you, too."

"Yeah, hi. Now, why did I hear Raine telling Shelby you're too busy to bother with family?"

"I didn't say that," he protested with a frown.

"Neither did she, but that's what I heard."

"Maybe you should clean your ears then."

"What are you doing tonight?"

Reyes fisted his hand in the cloth, resting it on the shining leather in front of him. "I have a few things to get done here, and some work to do on my jeep."

Dev's impatience sounded across the line. "Whatever that vague bullshit is, I'm willing to bet none of it has to be done tonight. You've been pulling away again, Rey, ever since brunch a couple of weeks ago. Either tell me what's going on or come on over and have dinner with us."

Reyes clenched his jaw, then blew out a rough breath. "The more time I spend with her, the more I like her."

"Raine?"

He rolled his eyes. "Of course, Raine. Who else would I be talking about?" In fact, he more than liked her, but admitting that out loud would make it too real. Too hard to move past later on.

"I thought you two were friends now?"

"You know damn well being friends with her isn't the problem." He raked a hand through his hair as he leaned back in his chair.

"Yeah, I do," Dev agreed.

"How the fuck did you keep Shelby at arm's-length when you were with her twenty-four, seven?" When he was being paid by her father to guard her, not sleep with her.

"We talked," his brother said with a grin in his voice. "There was *a lot* of talking. But honestly, taking time to get to know each other now can be a good thing for when you're free to act on what you're feeling."

"Free to act." Reyes snorted and shoved to his feet. "When exactly would that be? When she goes back to Texas? Or when she's out chasing Olympic gold?"

"I didn't say it would be easy."

"It won't be anything because it ain't happening, Dev. She'll go home, and I'll just be some guy who trained her for a few weeks. You all have a good night. I'll stick to working on my jeep."

aine sat on her cousin's back patio, sipping a glass of wine with Honor, Shelby, Mae, Celia, and Roxanna. Honor laughed at something Mae said, and Raine forced a smile to make it appear she'd been listening. Then she made herself pay attention. After brunch that first weekend, they'd all gotten together for drinks a few days later, and Shelby insisted they had to do it one last time before Raine went home to Texas.

The guys were across the street at Mae and Merit's house with the three kids. Well, all but Robert and Reyes. She was dying to know exactly what Reyes' plans were, but when she considered maybe he'd had a date, her stomach soured. It didn't matter that he'd kissed her senseless two weeks ago and avoided physical contact with her ever since, she didn't want to think of him with another woman. Like Jess's cousin's niece, maybe.

She made a face, then quickly smoothed out her expression when Mae lifted the bottle of wine to offer refills. Raine shook her head, sticking to her one-drink limit so she could drop Celia off at her house on her way back to the guest house in Aunt Janine's car. Honor took a refill, because all she had to do was walk upstairs to bed, and Rox and Shelby finished off what was left in the bottle, since their designated drivers were across the street.

While their small patio fire flickered, lightening in the distance drew her attention to the storm clouds gathering over the mountains to the west. Each flash illuminated the jagged peaks of the Rockies for a few seconds before they melded back into the dark sky. The storm mirrored her emotions lately. Bright flashes of hope quickly swallowed up by gloomy reality.

"We've got about an hour before that hits," Rox commented as the sky lit up again.

And it was already nine-thirty, Raine noted on her phone—in addition to the battery being low. "I should head out soon anyway. I'm not training tomorrow, but I still want to get down to the stables at a decent hour. I know I'm going to sound old, but usually I'm in bed before ten."

Honor snorted. "That's old? Between the bakery and Ava, Asher and I are eyeing the clock by eight every night. I might have two four a.m. bakers, but I still try to get there by six every morning."

"I always wake up when Robert gets up for his run at five-thirty, so I just head into the office early," Celia said. "Even on a Sunday, he still gets up for his run."

Raine heard the hint of annoyance in her oldest cousin's tone just as Mae raised her hand.

"Five-thirty here, too, and to the construction site by seven now that Merit takes Ian to school before taking Maverick to his studio for a few hours."

"Ditto with the clinic," Shelby chimed in.

Raine gave a wry grin. "So what you're all saying is seven a.m. is sleeping in?"

Amidst a chorus of *yeses,* Roxanna raised her glass. "I'm with you, Raine. I don't open the shop until eight."

She clinked glasses in solidarity with the brunette, and then sat back for another sip of wine as the fire crackled in the center of their circle. The emotion swelling in her chest now had her speaking past a lump in her throat. "I have to thank you guys for these nights. I've really enjoyed being here these past three weeks and getting to know everyone. And I pray my brothers find partners even half as awesome as all of you."

"I'm going to miss you," Shelby said with a pout. "I can't believe you're leaving in a week."

Neither could she. Truthfully, she was torn over going home. With Reyes camped out behind a brick wall as formidable as the mountains, it annoyed the hell out of her he wouldn't even try to be friends. She was sad the month was almost over, and yet she couldn't wait until she didn't have to see him every single day while her heart longed for so much more.

Saying it over and over doesn't make it true.

Still, she needed to keep repeating it, in hopes it would help her to stop wishing for what she clearly couldn't have.

"How's everything going with Reyes?" Roxanna asked.

Raine's stomach flipped, the psychic brunette's question too close to reading her mind. To admit things were strained would be an understatement, and invite questions she didn't want to answer. It would also invite confessions she was doing her best to avoid.

"It's fine. I'm sure he'll be glad to get back to his regular schedule."

Shelby leaned back in her chair and propped her feet on the brick edging along the fire pit. "Are you still helping him with the new thoroughbreds? What were their names again?"

"Saving Grace and Willow Moonlight. And yeah, that's been great."

Other than time with family, that had been the one bright spot over the past couple of weeks. Reyes may have been one hundred percent business-like in the process, but he'd gone over everything with her step by step, from picking the horses, assessing how to retrain them, the paperwork involved, and anything else she needed to know to get started.

Unfortunately, his knowledge and devotion had impressed her on a whole other level, making the distance he was forcing between them hurt even more.

"I love the names they come up with for those horses," Mae said.

"Me, too," Raine agreed. "In fact, I talked to Loyal earlier about helping me set up a business plan to start my own rescue when I get home."

"Seriously?" Shelby grinned when Raine nodded. "Wow—that's great."

They peppered her with questions until a side tangent changed the conversation, leaving Raine thinking about how she'd have to call Jessica at Retired Racers to see if she had any contacts in Texas, and if not, hopefully she could get a couple of horses from her. Or the trainer in California Reyes had mentioned earlier. Or, she could do what Reyes had done and take the time to visit some racetracks to make her own contacts. Horse people loved talking about horses.

It wasn't much longer before the approaching storm had her and Celia saying goodbye and heading home. A few minutes after she dropped Celia off at her house, Raine's phone sounded a severe weather alert for a tornado watch for the Greater Denver Metro area and surrounding suburbs until midnight.

By the time she turned into her uncle's winding driveway, the wind buffeting the car sent a small surge of apprehension along her spine. Things could get a little wild tonight.

She parked her aunt's car in the guest house garage, then tossed the keys and her purse on the island counter before plugging her nearly-dead phone into the charger. Thunder rolled overhead as she went to stand by the window to look out at the stables.

At nearly ten-thirty at night, the building was dark save for the lights shining from the second floor windows. The same lights that were on every night in Reyes' apartment. All night.

An ache throbbed in her chest, and she rubbed at the sensation. If he wasn't so determined to keep her at a distance, maybe she could've helped him like he'd helped her.

Vivid flashes of lightning revealed the trees swaying in the wind and uneasiness had her heading back to her phone to check the local radar. The estate was right on the edge of a red cell, but any indication of possible tornados were north and east a good thirty miles. Still, future cast showed they weren't out of the woods yet.

A deafening boom shook the house and ground beneath her feet—and everything went dark.

Raine jerked so hard she fumbled her phone, barely rescuing it before it crashed to the floor. Heart lodged in her throat, she spun to face the pitch-black living room with her phone clutched to her chest. That thunder had been so loud, she'd swear a bomb had gone off—

Bomb.

Reyes.

Her pulse revved like a freight train as she whirled

to look out the window again. Reyes was over there in the dark.

Alone.

She yanked her phone from the charger and ran out the door and across the yard as the angry clouds overhead let loose with huge drops of cold rain. By the time she reached the stables, her hair and shirt were drenched, but she only cared about making sure he was okay.

Slamming the barn door shut against the wind, she leaned against it, chest heaving as she sucked air into her tight lungs. "Reyes?"

A second louder call over the thunder received no response as the lightning pierced the darkness through the windows with an eerie strobe effect. Using the flashlight on her phone, she hurried up the stairs to his apartment.

Though she gave a brisk knock, she didn't wait for an answer before turning the handle. The door swung open easily. "Reyes? Are you up here?"

"Raine?" The relief in his voice was edged with panic.

"Yeah, it's me." She shut the door behind her as she shined her light across the room.

He pushed to his feet from where he'd been sitting with his back pressed against the kitchen cabinets. His chest was bare, and black sweat pants hung low on his hips. His hair was a rumpled mess, as if he'd been sleeping—or run his hands through it over and over.

Recognizing the hunted air about him, like the night in the pool, she guessed the second. Her heart thudded with sympathy when she saw him grip the counter with white knuckles.

Definitely the second.

"The storm knocked the power out," she said, striving to keep her voice casual. "I wanted to check on the horses."

His head snapped up. "Shit. Are they okay?"

"I came up here first." When his gaze met hers, she offered a quick smile. "I was hoping you'd come with me. It's a little creepy down there" —in the dark— "with the storm."

His Adam's apple bobbed hard, but he nodded. "Yeah."

When his deep breath sounded choppy as all hell, she started across the room. "Do you have any regular flashlights, or a lantern or something? My phone battery is barely at three percent."

He dropped his gaze to the countertop, his jaw clenched. He closed his eyes with a grimace, but then popped them open again as if he couldn't bear the darkness.

Raine was at his side by then, and he flinched when she reached out to firmly grasp his forearm. His gaze rose to hers, and her heart jolted at the dark torment in his eyes.

"Everything's fine," she said softly, the reassuring

words tumbling out as she gave a light squeeze of her fingers. "The power's out, that's it."

His muscles flexed beneath her hand. "I panicked. I have a flashlight in the drawer next to the sink. And I have my phone…" He paused, a frown creasing his brow as he swept his gaze along the length of the island counter. "It's still in the bedroom on the nightstand. I panicked."

The second time he said those words there was a note of angry disgust in his voice.

"You're not alone."

"I should've been better prepared."

She set her phone on the counter, deliberately facing the flashlight down. Then she reached her free hand up to his face to cup the side of his jaw in the dark, grounding him with her touch. "Maybe it's time to face this, Reyes. When you have a friend to help you through it."

His hand rose up to cover hers, pressing her palm to the rough stubble alongside his goatee. "We're not friends," he said gruffly. Achingly.

"Yes, we are. We have been since that night in the pool. Now, let's get the flashlight out of the drawer and check the horses."

When she lowered her hand from his face, he surprised her by keeping hold of it. He didn't say a word as he threaded his fingers with hers, just held on tight, and she did the same.

Lifting her phone with her free hand, she aimed the

light toward the drawer next to the sink. She noticed her battery was down to two percent as they moved together to dig out the flashlight. Once he clicked on the light, the beam glowed strong for a moment, then dimmed to half its strength.

When it flickered and dimmed more, Reyes shook it, cursing under his breath.

"Are there more batteries?"

He rummaged in the drawer. "No."

"Grab your phone, then. Mine's going to die any—" As if on cue, the screen went black.

"Mine's in the bedroom." He closed the drawer and turned, and she had to fight from leaning into him when the warmth of his bare chest brushed against her chilled arm.

All of a sudden he turned the weak flashlight beam on her. "You're all wet."

His surprise sparked a smile. "I am. Because there's rain to go with that thunder and lightning outside." And now that her brain was focused on her wet clothes, the chill of them had her shoulders shaking with an involuntary shiver.

"You need a dry shirt." He glanced down at his chest. "I should grab one, too."

Don't mind if you don't.

She let her gaze trail down over his tight pectorals and the defined ridges of his abs with a faint trail of light brown hair that disappeared into the waistband of his sweats. He robbed her of the chance to truly admire when he pulled her with him toward the bedroom.

Their destination sped up her pulse, but he released her hand to retrieve his phone from the nightstand. Another curse grated past his lips. "Mine's almost dead, too. I forgot to plug it into the charger before bed."

"I'm sure the power will be back on soon."

Even in the shadows from the dim flashlight, she could see his tight jaw as he swiped a white T-shirt from a bench at the foot of the bed, and then went to the closet to pull out a light gray button up shirt similar to the one she'd borrowed that day they'd taken a trail ride. The one she had forgotten to return at the end of the day, and then 'accidentally' forgotten each day since.

"This okay?" he asked.

"It's fine." She'd have to roll up the sleeves a half-dozen times, and it would reach halfway to her knees, but it was dry. "Thanks."

She took the shirt and walked the few steps to his unmade bed to toss it on the edge before reaching for the hem of her wet top. As her fingers gripped the material, she thought of him behind her, and the bed in front of her, and the fact he'd been lying in those rumpled sheets not that long ago.

Her heart rate ticked along even faster.

The dim light from the flashlight suddenly went crazy, bobbing all around the room before leaving her in even deeper shadows. When she glanced over her shoulder, Reyes stood near the door, T-shirt on, his back to her, flashlight pointed at the ceiling.

Was it terrible that she was disappointed he wasn't going to watch? And yet, her heart gave a hard thump of appreciation at his gentlemanly respect. Yet another little thing she loved about him.

Love.

Hmm. Don't go there.

She quickly exchanged wet shirt for dry, and then buttoned all but the top two buttons and rolled up the sleeves. The hem reached to mid-thigh on her damp jeans. Her bra was also damp, but already she was warmer. While his back was turned, she lifted the collar for a discreet inhale of fresh linen fabric softener. His other shirt had had a faint underlying note of the same scent, and she bit back a soft sigh.

A loud overhead rumble reminded her of the real reason she was standing in his bedroom, wearing his shirt. She scooped up her wet top and headed toward him. "All set. Let's go check the horses before the flashlight dies."

The light swung toward her, and she was thankful he kept it pointed down to keep from blinding her. He stilled for a long moment as he swept his gaze from the top of her wet head to the now soggy white canvas tennis shoes she'd worn over to Honor's.

He closed his eyes and tipped his head back, muttering as he turned to walk out of the bedroom.

Raine raised her eyebrows as she followed. She was

pretty sure he'd said something about being *"totally fucked,"* though she wasn't so sure she wanted to ask him to clarify.

He slipped on a pair of tennis shoes at the door, and they went down the stairs. A few of the horses were restless, but it didn't appear that any were having major issues with anxiety from the storm. Raine slipped into her tack stall for a handful of treats before taking time to pet and murmur softly to each one that bothered to stick their head over the stall doors.

After giving Taz a treat, she waited inside Fire's stall while Reyes checked the doors on both ends of the barn were secure against the wind. By now, the thunder had moved off into the distance, and the lightning flashes were only occasional even as rain still thrummed hard and steady on the roof.

Reyes' curse from the far end of the barn drew her around, and she rose on her tiptoes to see over the stall wall. She noticed it was pitch black on his side of the barn at the same time he called out, "Flashlight's dead. My phone's dead, too."

Hearing the strain in his voice again, she hurried out of the stall and down the aisle. A weak flash of lightning revealed his outline at the far door. When she reached him, he fumbled for her hand and squeezed tight. She moved closer, pulling her fingers free to slip her arms around his waist. His whole body was stiff as a board, muscles tight as if he was doing everything he could not to panic.

"I'm right here, Reyes. I'm not going anywhere."

His arms closed tight around her as his chest heaved beneath her cheek. "I fucking hate this."

"I know. Believe me, I know."

"I know you do." After a long moment, he murmured, "Thank you."

His bent head put his gruff voice right next to her ear. She shivered as the husky sound set off flutters of awareness deep in her belly. A steadying breath only made it worse. The scent from his shirt was magnified times a hundred from the oh-so-warm flesh and blood man in her arms. Fresh linen combined with his musky scent was a dangerously tempting combination.

She nearly groaned in pent up frustration, then rolled her eyes in the darkness. Here he was dealing with his own PTSD, and she was getting all turned on by how damn good he smelled.

And felt.

Except some of the tension had left his body, and all of a sudden, she felt the warmth of his lips and breath on her neck. The past couple weeks of suppressed yearning flooded forward to intertwine with the more tender emotions for this wounded man taking over her heart.

She turned her head with a helpless murmur, seeking his mouth with hers.

18

*R*eyes pulled back at the exact second Raine's lips met his. He almost gave in—God knew how badly he wanted to give in when he heard her second soft moan of protest—but it would be for all the wrong reasons. Or mostly the wrong reasons.

He didn't want her pity. Nor did he want to use her to deal with his fear even though his body was already half-hard in total approval of that plan. He couldn't let it matter that her voice and soft touch had a grounding effect that kept him from focusing on the dark. As long as she was with him, he could keep the panic at bay, and yet, he hated how weak that need made him feel. Even though she understood, he hated her seeing him shaking like a cowering dog.

He reluctantly felt for her hand, fitting her smaller palm against his. "Come on. I can take you back to the guest house."

"In this rain? Not a chance."

Her instant, firm refusal triggered a knee-weakening wave of relief.

"I'm waiting upstairs with you until the power comes back on," she stated. "Or the rain quits."

His chest tightened at the last bit she tacked on, and a knot formed in his stomach at the thought of her leaving before the power came back on. He didn't argue any further as he felt along the stalls to the stairs, because selfishly, he'd take whatever he could get.

In the apartment, he closed the door behind her before pausing a moment to picture the layout in his head. Dark or not, he needed to get some space between them. "You can have the bed. I'll take the couch."

When he led her toward the bedroom, she resisted. "I thought we could talk."

Talk. Dev had said he and Shelby did lots of talking. But that would only bring them closer.

Keeping Raine moving, he countered, "It's late."

"I'm not tired."

Neither was he, but—

They'd reached the doorway, and he steered her into the room, but when he would've backed away, she grabbed both his hands and pulled him with her.

"Raine."

"We can't talk if you're out on the couch and I'm in here."

"Ever consider that's the point?" It was a half-hearted protest at best.

"No." She tugged him forward. "Come on, are you really going to leave me in here all alone?"

He should. He really, *really* should. Yet, his feet were still following her to the bed. "You don't have to do this," he said gruffly.

"Do what?"

"Babysit me. I can deal with this."

"I'm sure you can. But why do it alone when you don't have to?"

He shrugged, then remembered she couldn't see him any more than he could see her. It was crazy how truly dark everything was. Forget the bedside lamp he usually left on twenty-four seven, with the power out and the storm blocking any moonlight, not even a ghost of a glimmer shone through the windows. No power indicator lights blinked from any appliances to soften the inky blackness.

And then he realized a second later, even crazier still was how his back and forth kinda bickering with Raine shifted the focus from the black hole of his fear—even when they were beating around the bush about that exact subject.

"I want to be here with you, Reyes. We don't even have to—whoops—that's the bed." Her voice sounded a bit breathless. She pulled harder on his hands for a moment, and his body collided with hers. "We can just lay here if you don't want to talk."

A great offer, but if he lay with her without talking,

he'd end up thinking of all the things he wanted to do with her.

Talking might be safer.

He disengaged their hands and stepped back, but didn't go any farther.

"*Or…*" she ventured, "you could tell me about what happened to you three years ago."

He'd rather think about all the things he wanted to do with her.

Rustling noises told him she was doing something, but he couldn't even see the shadows of her movement. His fingers clenched for a moment before he consciously relaxed them. Even if he could manage to scrape together every last little atom of willpower he possessed, it wouldn't get him back out to the couch, so he sidestepped around her, felt for the edge of the bed, and then sat while toeing off his shoes. Then he swung his legs up on top the comforter and scooted back against the headboard.

"I already told you what happened."

"I know, but—" The mattress dipped as she climbed up—right over him. "Oh. Sorry. I can't see anything."

He sucked in a breath when her hand brushed over his groin. He quickly reached to help her over to the other side of the bed and encountered a whole palmful of warm, bare thigh.

Holy shit—had she stripped down?

Heat seared through his veins as he jerked his arm

away and grabbed the top of the headboard to keep from reaching for her again.

"What did you take off?" he asked before he could help himself.

"My jeans were wet."

Which meant she was in his bed in just his shirt. He leaned his head back against the headboard as the semi he'd been trying to will away swelled to full mast.

Yeah, he was totally fucked.

She rustled around a bit more, adjusting the pillow by the sound of it. But then she scooted in close against his left side, and he stiffened when she tucked her shoulder under his arm, draped her arm across his stomach and pillowed her head on his chest. Her knee rested against his thigh—thank God, because if she'd draped it over him, he was pretty sure nothing could've stopped him from reaching down to haul her fully on top of him.

Reyes stared across the room in the dark, the headboard biting into his fingers as he gripped it tight while his pulse roared in his ears. Like earlier in the barn—and any other time he got too close—the airy, floral scent of her filled his senses and had him wanting to bury his face in her hair.

Talk about torture. Laying there on his bed with her pressed against him was worse than working with her with the thoroughbreds the past couple of weeks. He'd done his level best to keep everything strictly business, but in this moment—and if he was being honest, all the others before it—he was helpless against the tide of emotion he should resist at all costs.

Raine slid her hand up his chest to his face, her touch ghosting over his lips before shifting down just a bit. His pulse stumbled when she traced the line of his scar with her fingertip.

"Did this happen that day?"

He swallowed hard at the question and managed a slight nod and strangled sound of confirmation. She didn't press further, and after a long moment, he let out a pent up breath while lowering his arm to curve over her shoulder and arm. She snuggled closer, and his heart warmed, even as his gut tightened at the words rushing to the tip of his tongue.

But what was that stellar advice he'd given her weeks ago?

You gotta face what happened.

"It was supposed to be a routine sweep of an isolated compound. Intel said the place had been deserted for weeks." He paused as vivid memories flashed in his head like snippets from a movie trailer. "I led the way in initially, but we spread out to check the rooms, and one of my guys hit a trip wire."

Her palm flattened against his jaw, warm and comforting. Reaching up with his free hand, he pulled hers back down to his chest and held tight.

"I have vague memories of screams and yelling and then nothing until I woke up on the plane to Landstuhl in Germany. I couldn't see a damn thing."

"I can't even imagine how terrifying that must've been."

He could only squeeze her hand in affirmation.

"What about your team?"

A lump formed in his throat from both her asking about the others, and what had happened. "Neider—the guy who tripped the wire—didn't make it."

Her palm pressed over his heart. "I'm so sorry."

Reyes tightened his arm on her shoulder for a brief moment in acknowledgment of the husky emotion in her voice. "Hughes and Dice rode transport to Germany with me. They were both medically discharged because of their injuries."

"You weren't?"

He made a negative sound. "Once my vision came back, my injuries were all surface."

She shifted until he felt her rest her chin on the back of the hand she'd flattened against his chest. "Still, I don't think it's right they made you go back."

"I insisted on going back," he corrected.

"Why?"

He smiled slightly at the astonishment in her voice. "My team was still there. No way was I going to go home when I was still physically able to serve with them."

"And mentally?"

"Believe it or not, it was better there. After I came home is when things got worse."

"After you were away from your team?"

"Yeah."

A change in pressure on his chest told him she'd tilted her head. "Have you talked to anyone?"

"Dev. The horses. You."

The lamp on his nightstand clicked on.

Reyes blinked at the unexpected light and found himself staring right into Raine's hazel eyes. The hum of the refrigerator and other appliances seemed unusually loud in the suddenly awkward silence as their gazes held. He read sympathy in her eyes, not pity, and another raw, warm emotion that kick-started his pulse.

"Hi," she murmured softly.

His lips twitched. "Hi."

Her gaze dropped to his mouth, and in the space of one heartbeat, desire hit with a dizzying rush. The sudden hitch of her breath told him she felt it, too.

He lifted his hand to tuck her damp hair back and couldn't seem to help but let his touch linger on the soft, delicate shell of her ear. Of their own accord, his fingers slipped into her hair, burying deep for an anchor in his losing battle against rising desire.

She held his gaze steady as she pushed up and swung a leg over to straddle his thighs. He drew in a ragged breath, his body throbbing with need as he wished she'd settled a few inches higher.

Clenching his fingers ever so slightly in her hair, he drew her forward, his gaze zeroed in on her lips. Even with the move, he made one last token effort at doing the right thing.

"You know there are all kinds of reasons why this is a bad idea."

"Maybe." Hands braced on his shoulders, she leaned in until her lips were less than an inch from his. "But in this exact moment, there isn't a single one I give a damn about. You?"

Reyes couldn't even remember them, much less give a damn about them.

He answered with a little tug to close the distance between them and melded his mouth with hers. When her lips parted on a sigh, he angled her head and deepened the kiss with a bold stroke of his tongue. Her soft moan only drove him deeper, until they were both desperate for air. He sucked in a lungful while trailing his lips down along her throat.

He reached for the buttons on her shirt—*his* shirt—his heart thudding hard at the anticipation of revealing what lie underneath. Raine eased back, her hands lightly trailing over his forearms as he worked his way down. He caught her swift glance at the bedside lamp at the same time he realized earlier she'd removed her jeans *and* her bra.

Sweet Jesus.

"So, um, do you usually just leave the light on all the time then?" she asked.

He was busy taking in the exposed curves of her breasts. "Usually."

"And no one's minded?"

Reyes stopped on the second to last button and

looked up. "Do *you* mind?" She shook her head, but he noticed the corner of her lip caught between her teeth. "Raine, you can be honest."

"I don't," she insisted. Then she rolled her eyes with a slightly sheepish smile. "I guess I'm just curious if other women you've been with have been okay with sleeping with the light on. What do you tell them?"

He tried to avoid answering by teasing, "Really? Right now, you're curious about other women?"

She frowned, and ducked her head. "I'm sorry. That was stupid to ask."

"No." He tucked a knuckle under her chin and raised her gaze to his. His heart thumped hard as he admitted, "I don't know if other women would be okay with it because I haven't been with anyone since before it happened."

Her eyes widened. "In three years?"

He lifted his shoulders, then let them droop as nerves rushed in. Until this moment, he hadn't really thought about how long it had been. Well, he had, but now he was suddenly worried about how long he'd last.

Raine palmed his face with a soft smile, then leaned in to gently press her lips to his. He started to lift up to deepen the kiss, but she eased back a couple inches.

"Do you trust me, Reyes?"

The suddenly serious question prompted his solemn nod—until she leaned over and switched off the lamp. His pulse revved like crazy, and three years of conditioning had him tensing beneath her.

She leaned in again, her lips brushing his before raining soft kisses over his face. After a moment, his breathing eased, and he began to anticipate where the next one would fall.

"You good?" she whispered.

"Mm-hm."

"Good." *Left eye.* "Don't think of the dark." *Scar.* "Just feel." *Forehead.*

By now, she had his full attention, and with her body against his, *"Just feel,"* was an easy order to follow.

He parted the sides of her unbuttoned shirt and skimmed his hands up her rib cage to her breasts. He loved the weight of the firm globes filling his palms, and when he circled her hard nipples with his thumbs, her mouth settled over his again. A throaty hum vibrated her lips against his before he opened to the bold probe of her tongue.

A moment later, she shifted so her breasts were right in his face, the movement an unapologetic demand for him to take her in his mouth. He loved that she wasn't shy, and as she arched over him, her hips riding his as he sucked on one breast, then the other, he asked, "Tell me what you want, Raine. What do you like?"

"I want you," she breathed. Her fingers clenched in his hair, and she widened her legs, bearing down over his erection. "All of you."

His body pulsated in eager response, but if he buried himself in her right now, he'd likely be finished in a few desperate strokes.

So he stripped off the shirt and her panties, then flipped their positions. As he bent his head to swirl his tongue around one nipple, she skimmed his T-shirt up his back, her light touch a torturous tickle. A quick reach dragged it over his head, and he tossed it aside.

Her hands moved to his chest and he enjoyed the sensation of her exploring fingers before it became impossible to resist the temptation of her body laid out beneath him. Her muscles were firm and toned from years of riding, yet her skin seductively silky soft.

He took his time worshiping her breasts, then kissed his way farther down, past her navel, to the sweet spot that had her moaning his name minutes later. He wished he could see her face as she came apart beneath him, but wouldn't trade a moment of this with her for anything.

She drew in a deep breath when he moved up to lie beside her. "I'm not complaining," she said, "but I think you got that backwards."

Despite the smile in her voice, Reyes paused mid-reach for a condom in his night stand. "Things haven't changed that much in three years, have they?"

She laughed. "I was supposed to give *you* a good memory of the dark. Something to help after I…"

His chest clenched at where that sentence had been going before she trailed off. "After you're gone?"

Her soft sigh was full of regret. "Yeah."

He took it back. He would trade this one night for a lifetime of forever with her.

But that wasn't an option. She had to get back to her

life, and a career that included riding for Olympic gold. He would never ask her to give up her dream.

Reyes brushed his knuckles over her cheek before kissing her with all the pent-up longing of the past few weeks and what was to come in his future. Somewhere in there they stripped off his sweats and boxer briefs, and she nearly killed him with the soft explorations of her hands.

As her fingers circled his hard flesh and caressed up and down, his hips bucked in response. He reached down to close his hand around hers, applying torturous pressure before pulling her away.

"I need to be inside you," he rasped.

He rolled on the condom, then positioned himself at her entrance. In the faintest of light filtering in from the outside yard lights, he saw her lips part on a soft gasp when he slid into her tight heat. A low groan of pure pleasure rumbled from deep in his chest as he buried his face in her hair.

Holy fuck, I don't remember it ever feeling this good.

A soft laugh whispered over his ear. "I'd love to take the credit, but that's just because it's been a few years."

"Did I say that out loud?" he asked.

"Yeah." Raine arched beneath him, her hips urging him to move.

After a few strokes, another moan left his lips when she matched his rhythm. "Take the credit—it's truly all yours."

Her hands in his hair drew his mouth back to hers. "How about it's ours?"

He didn't agree or disagree as a tingle started at the base of his spine, urging him faster. He fought hard to hold on until she came first—or with him—but his control slipped fast. "Raine...I...I can't..."

"It's fine," she bit out, her nails biting into his back. "I'm good. Oh, God, Reyes, *so good.*"

Her inner muscles tightened around him. His climax barreled through him, and he let go as it carried him over the edge with her.

His pulse still beat crazy fast as he tried shifting to the side moments later. With her arms wrapped around him, her fingers threading through his hair at the nape of his neck, she made a negative sound and kept his weight over her body.

Emotion swelled in his chest, and he knew without a doubt he'd failed despite his best efforts. She'd given him this memory to hold onto in the dark, and in turn, she'd take his heart with her when she left. He wasn't so sure the exchange was fair—but he wouldn't take it back for anything.

Now, he just had to figure out how to live with only the memory as she rode her way to gold.

19

*S*unday morning, Raine woke briefly when Reyes murmured he was going to feed the horses, and then a short while later, he slid back under the covers with her. She couldn't remember the last time she'd stayed in bed past eight, and certainly not with a man. But he'd woken her with a kiss that quickly turned into so much more.

She wished she could spend the whole day with him right here, but reluctantly lifted her head from his chest to check the clock on the nightstand. "Brunch is in an hour. I should get back to the guest house to shower and get ready. You want to meet me up there?"

There was a beat of silence before he pressed a kiss to her shoulder, then rolled over to sit up on the other side of the bed. "I'm not going to brunch."

Raine sat up, holding the sheet to her chest. "You're not?"

Back still to her, he shook his head as he pulled on his briefs and a pair of jeans. "I got other stuff to do."

Surprised by his short tone, she frowned in disappointment—and hurt—while reaching down for the button up shirt he'd given her in place of her wet top. As she slipped it on and secured the buttons, it took all her willpower to not demand exactly what *stuff* was more important than making the most of the time they had left?

"You want coffee?" he asked on his way to the door.

In what, a to-go cup?

Biting back the snark, she said, "Sure. Thanks." Then she sat dumbfounded after he left, wondering what the hell had happened in the past thirty seconds?

Life had made a seismic shift last night and then settled into a new reality this morning. But maybe it had only been for her. Maybe he hadn't felt the same connection when they made love, and she was the only one who wanted to use the rest of her stay to figure out how they could have a future together.

Swallowing past the lump in her throat, she pulled on her panties, grabbed her bra and now dry jeans, and headed for the bathroom right next door to his bedroom. She shot Reyes a quick look in the kitchen. He had his back to her, his hands braced on the counter in front of the sink, his shoulders hunched as he stared out the window overlooking the white-fenced pastures. As if the weight of the world was suddenly resting on those broad shoulders.

She wanted to ask what was wrong, but chickened out and turned back toward the bathroom—until she spotted her top from the night before draped over one of the island stools to dry. Probably better to wear that across the lawn, just in case any of her cousins arrived early and saw her crossing from the barn to the guest house.

She was halfway across the living room to retrieve the shirt when footsteps pounded up the stairs from the barn. She jerked to a halt as a loud knock rattled the door.

"Rey? You in there?"

He spun around from the sink at the same time the door swung open. His brother pulled up short when he saw the both of them.

"Geezus, Dev, you could wait for me to get the door," Reyes grumbled as he came around to the other side of the counter.

"We were looking for Raine," he shot back, his gaze swinging from one to the other.

Heat seared her face as he clearly took in the whole picture with Reyes in just jeans, and her in just his shirt.

"You two really should answer your damn phones."

Hers sat on the island counter, completely forgotten after their trip down to check the horses. "My battery died."

"Mine, too," Reyes said.

"You should've charged them as soon as the power came back on," his brother advised. He shifted his attention back to her as more footsteps sounded on the stairs. "Shelby's been trying to call you since last night, and your *father* is looking for you."

Her stomach dropped out from under her at the same moment her dad appeared in the doorway. When had he gotten here?

Relief etched his features as he entered the apartment. "Thank God you're okay, honey. No one could reach you after the storm, and I didn't know what to think when you weren't at the guest—"

He stopped and broke off abruptly, his gaze sweeping down to where Reyes' shirt ended at mid-thigh as she clutched the rest of her clothes in her hands. Heat prickled along the back of her neck as her dad's expression darkened.

Reyes had moved to stand in front of the counter, and her dad pivoted to glower at him. "What the hell is going on here?"

Raine took a step forward. "Dad—"

He cut her off with a jerk of his hand. "I wasn't talking to you."

Her eyes widened at his furious tone. She went from feeling the need to explain to being royally pissed off. "Well you should be," she retorted.

Dev backed toward the door. "I'm just going to go let Shelby and her parents know you're okay."

Her dad's glare didn't waver from Reyes. "You sonofabitch. I paid you to be my daughter's trainer, not sleep with her."

Reyes stood stiff as a board. "With all due respect, sir, you haven't paid me a dime."

"Is that supposed to make this better?"

"No, but—"

"I'll have your job for this."

Raine's heart lurched as she took a quick step forward. "Knock it off, Daddy. Reyes didn't do anything wrong."

"He took advantage of the situation."

"He certainly did not." She shot a glance at Reyes to see his jaw clenched as tight as his fists. "I am a grown woman. I make my own choices."

"Looks to me like you're still making the same *bad* choices. I would've thought you'd learned your lesson by now."

White-hot heat speared through her at his words. She couldn't believe he would throw that in her face in front of Reyes—in front of *any*one. It had been years ago. She'd been eighteen and naïve. She *had* learned her lesson, which is why she knew what she and Reyes had was different.

Her gut clenched when she saw him frowning at her, and she shook her head at her dad. "That's not fair."

"I don't give a damn what you think is fair." He pointed to the door. "Put your clothes on and go pack your stuff. We're going home."

Disbelief spiked her anger. "I'll go home when I'm ready."

179

His furious brown gaze bored into hers. "Are you having any more trouble with the jump?"

"No. I told you, Reyes helped me work through it and—"

"Then you're ready. Besides, it's time you got back to competing. There's an event in New York in two weeks. I have you all signed up."

She blew out an irritated breath. "You should've asked me first."

"Why? This is your job. You need to get back to it."

"You're the one who made me come here, so don't blame me for being away." She stole a glance at the still silent Reyes and then faced her dad once more. "I don't want to leave yet."

"Because of him."

Yes. Him, and so much more. "Because it's *my* life. You're my dad, not my boss."

He gestured to the door as if he hadn't even heard her. "Go pack, Raine. *Now.* I will meet you at the guest house after I've spoken with Mr. Torrez."

"No." She crossed her arms. "And I'm not going to New York, either."

He stared at her for a long moment, his frustration palpable. "Who the hell do you think pays for everything? As long as my name is on the checks, you will do as I say."

"Fine, then I quit." The moment the words left her mouth, shock reverberated through her system. Her stomach fell like a lead balloon. Where had that come from? She'd always pushed back to some extent, but usually gave in after token protest.

Her dad's dark eyebrows shot toward his hairline. "Excuse me?"

A few simple words would take it back.

No.

Not this time. This is too important.

The eye-opening revelation slammed home. Nothing had ever felt this momentous. For once, she knew exactly what she wanted—*Reyes*—and she wasn't backing down.

A flood of relief buoyed her heart with joy and shored up her determination. She breathed deep, then lowered her arms and squared her shoulders while meeting her father's gaze. "I said, *I quit.* I'm done with competing. No more events. Find someone else to boss around, because I'm done."

Her dad gaped at her in shock. "What about the Olympics?"

Uncertainty skipped her pulse, but then it steadied. If giving up the Olympics was what it took to be with Reyes, so be it.

"Raine," her dad implored, "You can't do this."

"Watch me." And she marched out of the apartment to cross the lawn in nothing but Reyes' shirt.

$\mathcal{R}$eyes stared dumbfounded as Raine swept from the room. She didn't mean that. No way could she just give it all up. In fact, he was pretty sure she hadn't meant to say something so drastic at first—he'd seen the surprise on her face before she'd doubled down.

"This is your fault."

He shifted his attention to her father. The man's furious gaze threatened to incinerate him on the spot. "Sir—"

"Cut the bullshit, son. If you had an ounce of respect for me or my brother, you wouldn't have seduced my daughter."

He did his best not to flinch at the accusation. It had been the other way around from the second he'd met her—even all those years ago—but he wasn't about to tell her father *that*. Besides, she hadn't done any of it on purpose.

"She's a fully consenting adult," he said stiffly.

"You took advantage of your position with her."

"It wasn't like that at all." He shifted his stance and glanced out the door before meeting the man's gaze once more. "I care for her, sir."

"Isn't that nice," he sneered. "You'll be happy to know she has a history of *caring* for her trainers, too."

The implication sunk in deep to sour Reyes' gut. He frowned in the direction of the guest house. Was he just another guy on a list of guys for her? Was this something she did despite her proclaimed aversion to casual relationships? Or, had that simply been a line?

"Didn't know that, did you?" Mr. Diamond asked.

He clenched his jaw at the man's superior tone. Doing his best to ignore the crushing hurt bearing down on his chest, he asked, "What do you want from me?"

"End whatever it is that's going on—and end it for good. You've seen her ride. She's got gold in her future."

"I agree."

"Then you can't let her quit." The man's voice took on a desperate tone. "It's been her dream to ride in the Olympics since she was a little girl. If she gives that up because of some foolish notion there's something between the two of you, the time will come when she hates you for robbing her of that dream."

Wow. The guy knew how to get right to the heart of

it, didn't he? And yet, Reyes couldn't disagree with one word he said, or the apparent place it came from in the man's heart. It was hard to fault him for protecting his daughter's dream.

Besides, he'd been struggling with how to distance himself so he could deal with her leaving. Didn't this just provide the perfect fucking opportunity?

"Do this," her father added, "and I won't ask my brother to terminate your position. I'll even add a nice bonus to your paycheck."

Reyes jerked his gaze up, jaw aching. "I'll talk to her, but not because you just threatened my job, and most definitely not for your fucking money. You can get the hell out now."

Surprise flickered in the man's eyes, but then he left with a solid thump of the door.

As soon as he was alone, Reyes scrubbed his hands over his face and then turned to pound his fists on the counter, stopping just short to lightly tap the surface. So many emotions danced right in front of him, fighting for the upper hand. Anger, frustration, hurt, disbelief.

One rolled into the other until they coalesced into a howling cyclone that made it hard to breathe, much less think. The only thing that made sense was getting it over with sooner rather than later.

After a shower, he pulled on a T-shirt, jeans, and boots, then saddled Taz before heading up to the guest house. He knew without a doubt he was going to need some therapy the moment he walked away from her.

His heart thundered in his ears as he approached the door with heavy feet. When Raine answered his knock, the distress in her hazel eyes stole what little breath he'd sucked past the vice pinching his chest. He barely managed a gruff, "Hey," as he handed over her forgotten phone.

"Hi. Thanks." She stuffed the phone in her back pocket with a strained smile and stood aside to let him in. "I am so sorry about earlier."

"You don't owe me any apologies."

"I'm still sorry you had to go through that. My dad was a jerk."

No argument from him—though he very grudgingly admitted he understood the man's motivation even though he'd offended the hell out of him with the execution.

Raine shut the door and turned to face him. He couldn't keep his gaze from devouring her shower-damp hair and the beauty of her makeup-free features. She wore a filmy, peach-colored shirt, and a pair of white shorts that left her legs bare. Barely an hour ago, they'd been wrapped around him as he selfishly stole one more memory to hoard for later.

"Can you frickin' believe my father?"

Reyes grimaced as he glanced at the floor, then raised his gaze to hers. "He's right. You can't quit."

Surprise whisked across her face. "I can, and I did."

He shook his head. "You can't give up on your dream."

"What if it's not *my* dream?"

"What?" he asked with a frown.

She shrugged, her gaze shifting toward the French doors leading to the pool. "I don't know. When I think about the Olympics, I'm not sure who wants it more, me or my dad." She gave a short laugh. "Actually, my dad does, because I quit."

A spark of hope flared bright. If it was her father's dream, did he really have to do this?

Yes. She'll end up hating you.

The spark sputtered out. "I've seen how hard you work, Raine. You have to follow this through. Maybe your dad does want it more than you, but you still want it."

"I'm not so sure about that anymore."

And that right there cinched it for him. She wasn't sure she wanted it, but that also meant she wasn't sure she didn't. "You have to go home."

She shook her head with a frown. "I want to be here with you."

His heart kicked in his chest at her declaration. He hadn't wanted to use the next thing, but didn't see any other way. "Is that what you say to all your trainers?"

"What?" Her eyes widened, then narrowed. "What did he tell you?"

"That you have a history of…getting involved."

"It happened one time—*one*—and it was years ago. I was young and stupid, and he *did* take advantage."

"Your dad made it sound like more than that."

"Of course he did. He wants me to go home, remember?" Fury shook her voice. "I dated some after that, and had one somewhat serious boyfriend about two years ago, but that's it. That makes you the third guy I've ever been with, so whatever my dad told you, it isn't true. I would hope you'd believe me over him."

His heart soared, then took a dizzying nose-dive. *Shit*. That blew that angle. Which left him with the worst option of all. The one that would hurt the most.

Before he could form the words to send her away, her expression softened as she moved closer and took his hands. She tipped her face up, her eyes full of a warmth that squeezed his chest and made it hard to breathe.

The corners of her mouth trembled before she declared, "I love you, Reyes."

His heart lodged up in his throat. The emotion shining in her eyes matched what had been building inside him and solidified last night when she loved him through the darkness.

"I've had a thing for you since the summer we visited when I was fifteen, but these past few weeks, getting to know you, and last night..." Her cheeks flushed, and she ducked her head with a sheepish, almost shy smile. She squeezed his hands and looked up again. "I've always done what is expected of me. What my dad wants. But now it's about what *I* want, and that's to stay here and do the horse rescue with you."

He closed his eyes as one second of pure joy was swallowed up by black misery.

Years from now, when she realizes what she gave up, she will blame you.

He could not be the one to steal her dream.

Reyes pulled his hands from hers and stepped back. "You're reading too much into last night," he said gruffly.

A tiny frown marred her brow. She stared long enough to make him squirm, then shook her head with defiant bravado. "I don't believe you didn't feel our connection. Look me in the eye and tell me you didn't feel anything last night. Right now. I dare you."

She could dare all she wanted. He wasn't a Diamond.

He forced a shrug. "It was good, of course, but it was never going to be more than the one night." No matter how much he wanted it to be.

Her expression fell. "How can you say that?"

"I never made any promises."

"No, but..."

Her eyes went all shiny, and she blinked hard as she spun away from him. He fisted his hands at his sides. He had to get out. Now.

To keep from reaching out for her, he strode over to open the door. "Go home, Raine. Go ride like you're supposed to."

"Is he paying you?"

He froze halfway through the doorway and saw

she'd faced him once more. "You know me better than that."

"I sure thought I did." She swallowed hard. "Especially since you said you don't sleep around."

The next words made him sick to his stomach, but he forced them out anyway. "Well, as *you* said, there's a first time for everything."

He hated himself the moment he saw the utter devastation in her eyes. Guilt spurred his feet out the door and back to the stables. He galloped Taz across the land moments later, wishing he could outrun the blackness chasing after his soul.

He'd had to do whatever it took to get her to go for the gold…even if it ripped both of them to shreds.

21

"Rey?" his dad called across the arena shortly before five p.m. "I'm heading out. You almost done out here?"

Reyes reined Willow Moonlight over a set of four caveletti and brought the mare to a halt at the fence. His parents had returned from their month long Europe trip a week ago. The day after Raine had gone back to Texas with her father.

"I'm going to work with her for a little longer, then get some time in on Stimpy."

His dad took off his Denver Broncos baseball cap, scratched his head, then resettled the cap. "You should come over for dinner tonight."

"I got some stuff to do around here."

"You said that the past three nights. Your mother is worried about you."

So was his dad. He could see it in his eyes, and it

was there in the tone of his voice. Because he wasn't putting much into maintaining the happy-go-lucky façade of the past few years. What was the point? He was miserable, and it wasn't worth the effort to pretend otherwise.

But that didn't mean he wanted to talk about it either. Any of it. His parents knew some of what had happened in their absence, but not all. Dinner would only bring questions he wasn't ready to answer.

"Maybe tomorrow night."

"No more maybes," his dad warned.

Reyes shrugged and backed up Willow. "Tell Mom I'm fine."

"You know I don't lie to your mother."

He didn't say anything else as his dad left and he wheeled Willow around. He would be fine—in about fifty years, when he was dead and didn't have regrets plaguing him every second of every day.

Since Raine had left, he worked from sunup to sundown. Then he lay in the dark in his bedroom, fighting for air until her memory slipped in to ease the tightness in his chest. He relived every moment of that night with her in his arms until he fell asleep—which brought on a whole new form of torture.

His subconscious brought her to life in his dreams. He heard her laugh, saw her beautiful smile. That flicker of annoyance in those greenish-brown eyes of hers when he pushed her buttons. The flash of desire when he pushed *other* buttons. He filled his senses with the subtle flowery scent of her shampoo. Felt the silk of her pale skin as he caressed her curves. Tasted the sweetness of Raine on his lips and his tongue.

He inevitably woke up hard, his body pulsating with need as reality rushed in to chill his soul for another day.

After Reyes finished in the barn, the sun was long gone, and he wearily climbed the stairs. He ate a bowl of cereal standing by the sink with the TV playing on the other side of the room. Then he grabbed a beer and slouched on the couch. The show on the screen didn't interest him in the least, so he lifted the remote to shut it off. A few minutes later, he drained the beer and set it on the end table before reaching to turn off the lamp.

His breath gave that familiar, hated catch in the darkness, but he sought out Raine in his mind. Therapy and torture all in one.

Instead of that last night they'd spent together, his memory took him to their first day in the ring.

"I'm done. I'm going home."

"So, you're not only afraid of the jumps, you're afraid of me, too."

"I'm not afraid of you, I just can't stand you."

"Whatever you gotta tell yourself."

"You were a jerk last summer, and you've been a jerk since I got here last night. It's taking everything I have not to smack you right now."

His surprised laugh echoed in his head. *"Really?"*

"Yes, really."

"By all means then, go ahead. I dare you."

And she'd taken the dare and smacked him. Hard enough that the memory made his cheek sting even now. He raised his hand to his face as her unapologetic voice echoed in his head.

"Don't dare a Diamond, 'cuz we don't back down."

Another scene flashed—this time as they floated only inches apart from each other in the pool.

"How about we compromise? Tell me why you don't like the dark, and I'll tell you about the accident."

Another leap; another memory. At the pool again, but after that inferno of a first kiss that nearly made him lose his mind.

"You're seriously mad? I'm trying to do the right thing."

"The right thing would've been to not make me think you wanted this in the first place."

"I do want you, Raine. More than I've ever wanted anyone before. But I need this job. I need to be here."

But did he really need to be *here specifically* anymore? He was sitting in the dark by himself. And though he felt uptight and restless, he knew it had more to do with the subject of his thoughts than not being able to see.

Dealing with the dark had gotten easier each day—missing Raine had not.

"Don't dare a Diamond, cuz we don't back down."

Well, neither did a Torrez—unless he was a complete idiot.

His stomach churned with a sinking feeling just as a sharp rap on the door made him jump.

"Rey?"

Recognizing his brother's voice, he sat up straighter as he called, "It's open."

The door swung inward. With the light from the stairs at his back, his brother's front was in shadows. "I didn't think you were here."

"Then why'd you come up?"

"Saw your jeep." Dev leaned a shoulder against the doorjamb and crossed his arms. "You're in the dark."

"Can't put nuthin' past you, bro."

After a beat of silence, his brother repeated, "You're *in the dark.*"

As if he hadn't gotten the significance of the words the first time around. Because, you know, it was only *his* PTSD.

"Yes, I'm in the dark, Dev. Apparently in more ways than one."

"What does that mean?"

He winced. "Nothing." Schooling his features, he shifted to flip on the light, then arched his brows at his brother. "What are you doing here?"

"Dinner with the Diamonds."

"Hmm." He rose and swiped up his empty bottle to go toss it in the recycle. "Want a beer?"

Dev shut the door and raised his hand in a staying gesture. "No, thanks. We're heading home soon. I saw the lights off and the jeep here, and thought I'd check in."

Reyes moved forward to brace his palms on the island. "You've checked. All good."

His brother walked over to face him across the counter. "Or somewhat better, it would appear."

"Sure."

"Except I got a call from Dad earlier. He said you've been burying yourself in work. Like when you first got home."

So Dad sent Dev.

He wanted to be annoyed. Instead, his chest tightened at the fact they cared. Not that he ever doubted they did.

"Thing is," Dev continued, "unless you've started seeing a therapist about your PTSD, the only thing different I'm aware of in the past month is a certain Diamond up here for training."

Reyes dipped his head, staring at the counter as he traced his finger along one of the black veins in the marble-like top. He didn't want to admit his stupidity, but it was going to come out sooner than later.

"She told me she loved me."

"And?"

He glanced up. "And I sent her home."

"That much is obvious. I meant, and *how do you feel about her?*"

"I love her."

"Then why send her away?"

"She was going to stop competing. Give up her dream of riding in the Olympics. I couldn't let her do that. She would've come to hate me."

Dev nodded. "Maybe. So why didn't you go with her?"

"I didn't think it was an option." He gave a wry smile. "At the time anyway."

"And now?"

"It's definitely an option."

His brother smiled. "Good." He pulled his phone from his pocket, typed a message, and then reached to put it away again. "I'll take that beer after all. Let's sit down and figure this out."

One week later, Reyes followed Shelby and Dev into the arena complex in New York. A myriad of people milled about near concessions on the right, and through a wide opening front and center, he caught a glimpse of sand and jumps. Riders trotted and cantered past as they warmed up their mounts.

"Uncle Matt said he'd meet us by the left side— there he is."

Reyes had already spotted the signature Diamond dark hair. His brother's hand landed on his shoulder for a quick squeeze. "Good luck."

He gave them a nervous smile, then strode over to where Raine's father waited. The man's expression tightened when he made eye contact, and his whole body stiffened.

Reyes willed his pulse to settle down while extending his hand. "Mr. Diamond, we haven't been formally introduced. Reyes Torrez."

He looked down, hesitated, then accepted the handshake. "Matt's fine."

The older man's tone sparked surprise. It wasn't anywhere near as confrontational as his rigid body language suggested it would be.

"What are you doing here?" Matt asked.

Her father stood a good two inches taller than him. Reyes lifted his chin slightly to meet his gaze. "I love your daughter, sir."

"And she loves you."

"That's what she told me."

He frowned toward the arena. "So you're here to take her back with you."

A statement, not a question, and it was full of resignation.

Reyes shook his head. "I'm here to support her in whatever she wants to do."

Matt's gaze met his once more, surprise mingling with hope. After a long moment, he nodded. "She's about to ride. Let's see how she does."

22

*R*aine hadn't spoken one word to her father on the way home to Texas, nor any time they crossed paths in the two weeks prior to their flight to New York for the Grand Prix event in which he'd signed her up to compete. She almost didn't go, but having sought solace with Diamond Fire for countless hours out on the open Texas range to keep herself from wallowing, she felt closer to her mount than ever before.

He deserved the chance to jump. A ride of redemption.

She knew it sounded ridiculous—he had no such awareness—but she wanted to show the world they were stronger than ever after their fall last year. With a wry twist of her lips, she tugged at the hem of her fitted black jacket and smoothed a stray hair back into the severe knot at the nape of her neck. So, maybe it was better said as *her* ride of redemption.

And, based on the nervous excitement tingling in her body, a way to test herself as well. After they'd arrived last night, she'd taken a good hard look at her life and realized she needed to figure out her future for herself. She didn't want to just go with what her dad expected, or ride because Reyes had broken her heart and she had nothing else to do. She certainly wasn't going to ride because *he* told her to.

No. It was time she decided exactly what *she* wanted.

Reyes.

She ignored the whisper of her aching heart and refused to allow thoughts of him to mess with her focus. Having already warmed up in the schooling ring after last minute advice from Charlie, she sat astride Fire to watch the other jumpers with a critical eye while waiting for their turn.

She knew most of them from the Grand Prix circuit last year, and they were all so good. No, they were better than good. The best of the best.

Her stomach got a little queasy with the realization she used to be one of them.

No—I still am.

The affirmation resonated deep in her soul, which meant she had a lot to prove to everyone today.

Seeing they were up next, Raine closed her eyes and visualized the course walk-through again. Once they made it over the vertical at the mid-way point, they'd be fine. She just needed to make sure she didn't seize up before then. Or more importantly, *at* the jump.

"Do you trust Fire? Let him take you over it."

Her pulse skittered at the vibrant sound of Reyes' voice in her head. She did trust Fire. And, despite Reyes breaking her heart, she still trusted his advice when it came to her horse. They'd get through this as a team.

A deep breath quieted the white noise in her head enough for her to register her name and number had been announced. Diamond Fire pranced his way into the arena with an excess of energy that stirred the crowd. Raine mentally blocked out the noise, leaned forward with a murmured, "Let's do this, boy," and off they went.

She let years of practice and experience take over, and the second Fire cleared the first jump, a surge of exhilaration cleared her nerves. She'd argued with Reyes she wasn't so sure she wanted the Olympics, but all it took was that one set of rails here in competition to cement her certainty.

She wanted gold as much as she still wanted him. She wanted both.

Moments later, they sailed over the vertical as if it were mere inches, and after the final combination, the crowd roared as Fire cantered over the line. A quick glance at the board revealed no time or jumping faults. She pumped a fist in the air as the announcer confirmed she'd move on to the jump off with the current leader, and any additional riders who qualified.

She exited the arena and dismounted as Charlie took hold of the reins.

"Great job out there."

"Thanks," she undid the strap of her helmet and handed it over to hug Fire's neck. "He did amazing, didn't he?"

"You both did," her father's voice said from directly behind her.

Her stomach gave a little lurch as she turned to face her dad.

"I'm proud of you, honey."

Her anger over Colorado had dulled some, and now her certainty during the ride confirmed he'd done what he thought was best for her. Then she noticed tears in his eyes and emotion clogged her throat as she stepped forward to wrap her arms around his waist. "Thanks, Dad."

"I'm sorry about the last few weeks." His hand smoothed over her hair as his chest expanded on deep breath. "Whatever you decide to do, Raine, I'll support you."

She leaned back with a frown of confusion. "Whatever I decide to do?"

He loosened his hold and stepped aside. "Someone's here to see you."

She followed his gaze past the people milling about. When she saw Reyes leaning against the back wall, her heart lodged up in her throat and swelled with joy. It took a moment to register that Shelby and Devante stood with him. Her cousin offered a smile and a wave as they started forward without Reyes.

Her heart raced the whole time she gave them each a tight hug and distantly accepted their congratulations on the ride. All the while, she was hyper aware of the tall, gorgeous man a mere twenty feet away instead of however many states lay between New York and Colorado.

A stolen glance skipped her pulse at the sight of his tousled, dusty brown hair, those dark eyebrows, and his intense green gaze locked on her. He should've been nondescript in a plain black T-shirt and worn jeans, but Reyes Torrez was not a guy that would ever fade into the background. Not for her, anyway.

"She's not even listening to us," Shelby groused to her fiancé.

Raine turned her guilty gaze back to her cousin. "I'm sorry."

"Don't be." She jerked her head toward Reyes with a grin. "Just go."

She gulped back a surge of nerves and started toward him, her heart thudding hard with anticipation. As she got closer, words from the last time she'd seen him started to pour into her brain. Her feet grew heavy and a lump of renewed pain formed in her throat.

"You're reading too much into last night."

"I never made any promises."

She'd handed him her heart, and he'd shoved it back at her with no concern for the damage he caused.

Stopping in front of him, she crossed her arms. "Why are you here?"

He straightened from the wall, but left his hands in his pockets. "You and Fire looked great out there. It was an amazing ride."

"Thanks." She lifted her chin slightly as the announcer called the next rider. "You were right. I *do* want gold, and I'm not giving up until I get it."

"Good." He nodded solemnly. "I'm glad."

Someone bumped into her from behind, and she murmured a quick acknowledgment for their apology before turning back to Reyes. "You flew all the way here just to tell me you're glad?"

A crooked smile appeared and was gone just as quick. "I came to tell you I'm sorry, and that *you* were right."

About what? The anxiety in his eyes made her heart beat faster as she tilted her head and waited.

He eased closer, his gaze never wavering from hers. "I came because I love you, Raine, and I want to be here for you in any way you need me. Any way you *want* me. Because I pray to God you still want me."

The gruff emotion in his low voice weakened her knees, but she managed to keep from throwing herself into his arms. He didn't deserve for her to make it too easy after she'd spent weeks with an ache in her chest that had made it hard to breathe at times.

Arms still crossed, she dropped her gaze to his chest

while shrugging her shoulders. "Maybe you read too much into my words that day."

"Really?" he asked. "How does one not read everything into *I love you*?"

"You tell me," she shot back. "You're the one who told me to leave and walked away."

The hurt he'd inflicted seeped into her voice. She couldn't help glancing up to see his reaction even as she clenched her jaw at the revealing words.

Anguish darkened his eyes. "I thought it was what I needed to do." He grimaced slightly. "It *was* what I needed to do—I just wish I hadn't hurt you doing it."

"Why?"

"Because I knew I loved you then, but I could never ask you to give up your dream. I didn't want you to end up hating me someday."

"Better I hate you *that* day instead of letting me make my own choice?"

"I was damned either way." The frustration in his voice sent his hand up to rake through his hair. "If we'd had more time..."

If her father hadn't shown up they would have had another week. But that would've only made it harder for her to leave. Or, Reyes might have let her stay, and she very well may have ended up blaming him for the loss of her dream when it would not have been his fault.

Letting her think their night together meant nothing to him had been awful, but it sank in what he'd been willing to give up for her. It made her want to…smack him.

And kiss him.

23

*R*eyes was dying to reach out for her, to take her in his arms and kiss away the hurt or whatever else was keeping the distance between them, but he was also afraid to push too hard. He didn't know what he'd do if she couldn't forgive him.

"More time wouldn't have mattered," Raine said with a shake of her head.

Desperation nipped at his nerves, but he forced it back down. Like with the thoroughbreds, he needed to be patient.

"Everything was so...raw that morning," he said quietly. "But if we'd had more time, I would've realized you didn't have to stay. I could've gone with you, instead. I *can* go with you."

"But I'd never ask you to leave the place that brings you peace after what you've gone through. I know how much you need to be there."

Hope flared at the empathy in her words. At her use of present tense, not past.

"Not after you." He finally gave in to his need to touch her, reaching for her crossed arms, pulling a hand free to capture her fingers with his. "I haven't slept with the light on since you left."

Her soft smile added a splash of gasoline to his hope.

"I don't need the light anymore, but I do need you. If you'll still have me, that is."

She sighed and dropped her gaze to their joined hands, as if searching for the words she wanted to say. When she tried to pull her hand free from his, he panicked and held it tight while grabbing for her other one.

"I dare you to love me again."

"Really?" She laughed. "You think that's going to work?"

Her gaze lifted then, and his heart jolted at the tears in her eyes. "Don't cry. Please, Raine, I'll do whatever it takes," he vowed. "I'll even get on my knees to beg your forgiveness if you want."

She arched her eyebrows. "I'm going to want you on your knees at some point, but not right now."

Her teasing words sunk in and brought a flood of relief. They swept his mind to a place that sent his blood racing through his veins, and the sass in her eyes turned up the heat a good ten degrees.

"As for your dare…"

"Diamonds don't back down," he reminded.

When she pulled her hands free from his, his heart sank. But in the next instant, she reached up to lay her palms against his cheeks. "No we don't, but I can't take a dare to love you again when I never stopped in the first place."

This time, finally, the relief was complete. He rested his hands on her hips, allowing a small smile as he swallowed past the emotion in his throat. "I'm so sorry I messed everything up."

She rose up on her tiptoes. "You're forgiven. And guess I should thank you for making me figure out for myself exactly what *I* want."

"Gold."

"Definitely gold. And it'll be that much sweeter if you're with me when I win it. If you were serious about that?"

"Dead serious. I'll be right by your side." He slid his hands up to pull her flush against him while touching his forehead to hers. "I love you, Raine."

"I love you, too," she whispered back.

Happiness swelled in his chest as she wound her arms around his neck. He captured her lips with his and kissed her with everything he had.

Moments later, the announcer over the loudspeaker made him break the kiss. He cupped her cheek with one hand while grinning down at her. "You've got a jump-off to get ready for."

"I've got a jump-off to win," she corrected as they walked hand in hand to where everyone waited by Diamond Fire.

A half-hour later, he watched her do just that.

EPILOGUE

1 year later – first week of August

Grinning from ear to ear, Reyes blinked away the moisture blurring his vision as the Star Spangled Banner played for Raine Torrez and her fellow teammates atop the Olympic podium. At the end of the United States' majestic national anthem, the brilliance of her smile rivaled the sun when the team held their gold medals and flower bouquets above their heads in joyful triumph.

Her parents and four brothers had come for the whole two weeks, and Mark and Janine had flown in yesterday for the team event. Shelby and Dev had also planned on coming, but Shelby's morning sickness forced the couple to stay home and watch on TV. Last he'd heard, his brother had arranged for all the Diamonds in Denver to go to their house and watch their cousin go for gold.

At twenty-six, she was the youngest on the team and the only female. She and Fire had given the ride of a lifetime in the jump-off round to secure the US gold for the team event. Earlier in the week, they'd also won a silver medal in their individual event, and he'd never been more proud of anyone in his life.

"That's my wife up there," he boasted when a couple from two rows down glanced back at their loud, rowdy group. He didn't have to say for which team, because they were all proudly displaying the American flag.

It was still surreal to say those words, even though he often spun the ring on his finger while thinking of their wedding two months ago. She'd been radiant in her gown as she walked down the aisle, and then they'd ridden off into the sunset on Fire and Taz. Well, at least until they reached the reception tents erected on her parents' lawn, overlooking the horse pastures.

He'd suggested they wait until after the Olympics so she wouldn't have the stress of the wedding while training, but she'd insisted she wanted her name to read Raine Torrez in the history books. She'd been confident without being cocky, and now her dream had been fulfilled.

The medal ceremony drew to an end with the last of the pictures, and Raine met them all on the side of the arena for hugs and congratulations. Reyes stood back with Fire, giving her time with her family. She met his gaze over her mom's shoulder and mouthed, *"I love you."* He tossed her back a grin and a wink, letting her know he could wait for their moment. Yes, they'd been an inseparable team over the past year, but long before him, her family had been an integral part of her dream and they deserved these memories.

Later, after Fire had been brushed and pampered like a king, Reyes finally cornered Raine up against the wall of the stall. All the noise of the busy stables faded away as he pressed his body to hers and leaned in, forehead to forehead. She looped her arms around his neck and grinned up at him.

"You did it," he murmured.

"*We* did it," she corrected. "Fire and me and you."

"I'll take credit for one jump, and that's it. The rest was all—"

Her finger over his lips cut off his words. "Seriously, Reyes, this team wouldn't be the same without you. Thank you for everything you've done this past year."

"You don't have to thank me, Raine."

"No?"

"No."

"So, you don't want me to come to bed wearing nothing but my medals tonight?"

The image flashed in his imagination and sent blood rushing south in anticipation. "Well, when you put it that way, maybe I spoke too soon. You're right—you *should* thank me. Multiple times."

"I can definitely mount up for that," she teased.

He gave a low groan at that new image. "If we were the only ones in this barn, you'd be mine right now."

"I'm already yours. But…" She glanced around the stall, then rose way up on her tiptoes to peer out into the aisle. Meeting his gaze once more, she whispered, "If we tuck into this corner over here and keep quiet—"

"Don't tempt me woman," he growled before grabbing her sexy, breeches-covered ass to lift her up so she could wrap her legs around his waist.

Raine laughed softly as she leaned in to press her mouth to his, then proceeded to give him a very thorough preview of what was to come later. Fire's nudge against the back of his head broke up the kiss and he reluctantly lowered her feet back to the ground. Later couldn't come soon enough.

"What are you two still doing here?"

Charlie's voice had them both turning to see her trainer at the stall door.

"I know you guys have a room, go use it already."

Reyes left his arm around his wife as they stepped out into the aisle.

"I just wanted to make sure Fire was all settled in before we left," Raine said.

"Well, I'll take over for now, so you two go have fun. And Mike will be here with him tonight, so I'll see you at the party."

"Sounds good. Thanks."

As Raine led him out of the barn, Reyes said, "I like Charlie and all, but he is *not* joining our party tonight."

She giggled, then shot him an apologetic look. "Sorry, I didn't get a chance to tell you yet that there's a team celebration at nine. I kinda have to go."

He tamped down on his disappointment. "Of course you have to go." Because this could be a once in a lifetime experience, whereas he had her for the rest of their lives together. He was all for them taking in every moment possible.

"However…" She spun around to walk backwards in front of him while pulling her medal out from where she'd tucked it inside her shirt. Swinging it back and forth like a pendulum, she said, "We have about two hours to kill before we have to meet everyone for dinner. Got any suggestions?"

"You need a shower. You smell like horse."

"Gee thanks."

He flagged down a cab and held open the back door for her. "I love the smell of horse."

"Better."

"You also need a rub down after all your hard work today."

She paused to look at him over the door, a playful glint in her hazel eyes. "You know what they say about rubdowns?"

He smiled in anticipation. "No, what do they say?"

"One good rubdown deserves another," she quipped before sliding into the back seat.

Reyes groaned softly while silently vowing to give her the best rubdown of her life.

Approximately six weeks later

Raine reached for the door handle as Reyes put their new truck in park. She couldn't wait to get inside.

"Whoa—hold your horses."

She froze and turned to arch her brows at her husband of three months. "Is there a reason I have to wait?"

"Yes. A very good reason." He didn't say more as he opened his own door and got out, but he didn't need to. Over the past year, she'd discovered her man was quite the romantic, as well as a traditionalist.

She guessed right when he came around to get her door, then swept her up into his arms before she could step off the running board. Laughing, Raine draped one arm around his neck and pressed her other palm to his chest as he carried her up the large stone steps of the front porch.

"Welcome to our new home, Mrs. Torrez."

"Thank you, Mr. Torrez. And a happy birthday to you."

"Best birthday ever," he declared. He dipped his head to give her a lingering kiss before opening the door to carry her over the threshold. Then he lowered her feet to the floor and threw his arm over her shoulders as they stood in the doorway to gaze out at their eighty-six acre ranch, half an hour west of her uncle's place in Lakewood, Colorado, and fifteen minutes from his parents.

They'd signed the final closing papers barely an hour ago, and after calling the moving company, it wouldn't be long before the trucks and crews arrived with all their things. Estefan was delivering Diamond Fire and Raz-Ma-Taz the next day, giving them time to ready their stalls in the small barn set off to the left of the house. And then it wouldn't be long before rescue horses filled the other stalls.

"I still can't believe we found this place," Raine murmured, her arms wrapped around his waist.

Reyes pressed his lips to the top of her head. "It's going to be perfect once we get the new barn and indoor arena built."

He said *we* because he'd already insisted on heading up the building crew. Something about wanting to be able to say he had a hand in building their home. Or part of it, at least. Because, you know, traditionalist. And the more she thought about it, the more she loved the idea, too.

The sprawling ranch house had been built with the front facing southeast, which meant their backyard provided a magnificent view of the Rockies. It was morning now, and they had a ton of work to do, but she couldn't wait to enjoy the first of many sunsets with Fire and Taz out in the pastures that bordered the lawn.

"I want to help with the building," she announced.

"I'd never say no to that, but you won't have much time between training and events, and then add the rescue on top of that, too."

"Well…" Her pulse kicked up a notch as she drew back slightly. "I was thinking of taking a year off from the circuit."

He looked down, confusion all over his face. "I thought you were going for the Grand Prix championship? You and Fire are at the top of your game right now."

"We are, but I guess I should rephrase. I *have* to take a year off."

Confusion morphed into a frown of concern. "Why? What's going on?"

"Everything is fine," she reassured him while reaching for his hand. At least, she hoped he'd think it was fine. Pressing his palm to her flat stomach, she took a deep breath and said, "I'm pregnant."

Reyes' eyes went wide with shock as his gaze dropped. "What? Seriously?"

She nodded with a hesitant smile. "Seriously."

"But…we're still using protection."

Her stomach tightened. "Except for that one time after the gold medal ceremony. Remember?"

His gaze narrowed, and then he smirked. "Twice actually."

Right. Once in the shower, and the bed afterwards. Their little private celebration had made them late for dinner.

Realizing he still hadn't said anything specifically about her announcement, Raine said, "So, you're going to be a daddy in April. I'm due on the twenty-sixth."

As if the news had finally sunk in, Reyes blinked, and then a smile began to spread across his face.

Relief eased her nerves enough to bring back her smile. "You're good with this?"

"Hell yes, I'm good with it." He cupped his palm against her cheek, the love in his eyes deepening the green to her absolute favorite color. "How could you think I'd be anything but good with this?"

She grimaced with apology. "It's a little sooner than we'd planned."

"I'd say it's exactly as it's meant to be," he declared. "Making a baby on the day you won your gold medal couldn't be any more perfect. And finding out today— it's the best birthday present I could ever ask for." He looked down and palmed her stomach once more. "When did you find out?"

"My doctor confirmed it yesterday afternoon," she admitted. "I hated waiting, but I wanted to tell you on your birthday. I was going to do a whole thing with a cake tonight, but I couldn't wait any longer.

"I'm glad you didn't." All of a sudden he paused,

his gaze intense on hers. "Wait…are *you* good with this being sooner than we planned? With having to take a whole year off at the height of the season—"

She reached to press her fingers to his lips. "I'm one hundred percent good with it. I can't wait to be a mom."

Reyes caught her hand in his and pressed a kiss to her palm. "I noticed your excitement last night, but I assumed it was because of the house."

"Of course it was a little the house, but mostly it was the baby."

Dipping slightly at the knees, he wrapped his arms around her waist and lifted her in a bear hug as he spun them back out onto the porch. When he set her down again, he said, "I love that we're going to build onto this ranch at the same time we're growing our family almost as much as I love you, Raine."

"I love you, too. Isn't it crazy to think that my accident ended up with quite the silver lining?"

"I can't imagine what my life would be like if you hadn't come to Colorado to train last year."

She grinned. "You wouldn't be having nearly as much sex."

He laughed before tugging her in tight against him. "Speaking of, maybe we could—"

The blare of a horn cut him off as Dev's pick-up turned into the driveway, followed by two large moving trucks.

Reyes let loose a low growl of displeasure as she laughed. "Hold that thought, birthday boy."

The rest of the day flew by, until they fell into bed around eleven that night. Raine's attempt to treat Reyes for his birthday switched to him showing her slowly and thoroughly just how much he loved her. Afterwards, she snuggled close to his side, her head on his chest, his heart beating strong and steady in her ear.

A couple of months ago, she would've said nothing could top standing on the gold medal podium with her family cheering her on in the stands. After today, she had a whole new standard to judge by. Because this version of gold had the sweetest cherry on top.

Thank you for reading!

Do you want to help your favorite authors?

Reviews from readers help authors to be able to continue to write the books you love, so I really hope you enjoyed Reyes and Raine's story and would be thrilled if you'd leave a review where you purchased the book by clicking the link below. Copy/pasted reviews to BookBub and Good reads are golden, too!

Please review *Don't Dare a Diamond* at your favorite online retailer, as well as BookBub and Goodreads.

Thank you so much!

How can you make sure you never miss a new book?

JOIN Stacey's Newsletter and here's what you get:

*FREE bonus books

*New release announcements

*what's going on in my writer's life

*exclusive first-look bonus content

*cover reveals

*special sales

FREE reads!

Romantic suspense & Contemporary Romance
with heartwarming Happily Ever Afters

Sign up for my newsletter today!

ABOUT THE AUTHOR

New York Times bestselling author Stacey Joy Netzel is an avid reader of heartwarming, sexy, pulse-pounding romance, and she loves all movies with a happily ever after. She lives in Wisconsin with her family, a horse and some barn cats. She enjoys hiking, canning, and visiting her parents in Northeastern Wisconsin (Up North), at the family cabin on the lake. Travelling anywhere to the mountains to do some hiking is a bonus she wishes she could do much more often than every couple years.

She writes steamy romantic suspense, small town contemporary romances, and paranormal ghost stories with sexy, rugged heroes, and strong, resilient heroines. Colorado, Wisconsin, and Italy are favorite settings, and you can find them in her Must Love Diamonds, Romancing Wisconsin, Italy Intrigue, Welcome to Redemption Series, and Colorado Trust Series.

Website: http://staceyjoynetzel.com/all-books/

Hearing from readers is a very special thing for any writer, so pop in on FB and say "Hi!" sometime. And once again, reviews are always appreciated.

Thank you, and happy reading!
~Stacey~

facebook.com/StaceyJoyNetzelAuthor

bookbub.com/authors/BookBub

ITALY INTRIGUE SERIES

Enjoy a wild ride through Italy full of sizzling, sexy romance and a ton of adventure in this bestselling, award-winning series.

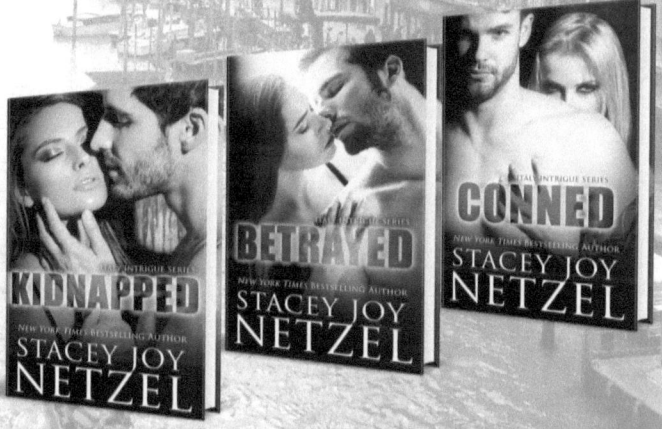

"Gripping romantic suspense in the Mary Stewart mold. Excellent Series!" ~ Helen

Passion flares as bitter enemies race to catch the stallion and win the ranch.

Catch the stallion—win the ranch...

chasin'
MASON

NEW YORK TIMES BESTSELLING AUTHOR
STACEY JOY
NETZEL

The writing style of Stacey Joy Netzel captivates me, and her art of telling a great romance story." ~ Danielle, reviewer

TRUST MAKES ALL THE DIFFRENCE WHEN LOVE AND DANGER COLLIDE

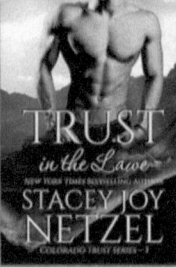

COLORADO TRUST SERIES

Set in the beautiful Colorado Rockies, this romantic suspense series won't disappoint with pulse-pounding action and steamy romance.

The individual books can be read and enjoyed as stand-alone stories, but why do that when you can enjoy the whole series?

"[**EVIDENCE OF TRUST,** Colorado Trust Series] *grabbed me from the beginning and I couldn't put it down. I loved Britt and Joel! I loved the action and the suspense and of course the romance!!*" ~ Angie, Amazon reviewer

TRUST BY DESIGN: "*Sizzling, sensual, spicy, sweet —Ms. Netzel dazzles her readers with a perfect romance in the midst of danger.*" ~ Casey Clifford, award winning romantic suspense author

"**TRUST IN THE LAWE** *is fun, suspenseful, and filled with characters that you will fall in love with. I have a great respect for Stacey Joy Netzel and the way she can write a romantic story with sizzle and spice that kept me absolutely addicted.*" ~ Val Pearson, You Gotta Read Reviews, 5 Stars

*"**SHATTERED TRUST** has everything a fantastic book should have, romance, suspense, betrayal, and humor in all the right places."* ~ Emily, Single Title Reviews

DARE TO TRUST: *"Thoroughly entertaining...I lost track of the time because I was so engrossed in the story."* ~ Diana Coyle, Night Owl Reviews

VOW OF TRUST: *"Strong characters with funny banter but underlying tension, suspense, and romance all in the same book. Right when you think you've figured it out she surprises you with a twist again!"* ~Ruby, Amazon reviewer

ILLUSION OF TRUST: *"Stacey Joy Netzel has a talent for creating characters that bring the story to life. I kept looking over my shoulder because danger was everywhere."* Rosemary, Amazon reviewer.

The COLORADO TRUST SERIES is available in ebook and print.